GIRL IN THE STORM

An Ella Porter Mystery Book 2

Georgia Wagner

Contents

PROLOGUE

She shivered but didn't say a word; her lips pressed so tightly together, she wondered if they were now turning from blue to white.

She heard whimpering in the dark and whispered, "Quiet... he'll hear you!" Another whimper, but softer now.

Maddie's shoulder scraped against the cold stone, and another burst of shivers shook her body. She couldn't see her friend in the murky cave behind her. But the small alcove in the face of the cliff served as a hiding spot. She continued to tremble, ears perked, listening intently.

Nothing. Only the whistle of the wind and the quiet shush of snow dappling gray rock. Her hands hugged against her legs, and she resisted the urge to lean forward and peer out from the dark towards the pale slopes beyond.

The snow had come too fast. They'd meant to return the previous day...

But then the monster had arrived.

"I-I think he's gone..." said the trembling voice behind her.

She shot another look in the dark but spotted nothing. The sound of her friend's voice was a disembodied thing. She felt her friend's hand against hers, strangely warm...

"Jas, wear your gloves!" Maddie admonished, shooting another look back and straining to see in the dark.

The outline of her friend stood out like a bleak wraith caught by the black of the cavern. Maddie shook her head in frustration but returned her attention to the opening in the mountain. The *only* opening. At least... so she hoped. They hadn't found another.

The two of them had broken off from the rest of their friends. After they'd heard the screaming. Had seen what *he'd* done.

For a day now, they'd been hiding.

Hungry, cold, tired, Maddie refused to back down. Her stubborn streak wouldn't allow it. "We're going to make it," she whispered to her friend, Jasmine. "I promise you. We will."

"Are you sure?" came the whispering, trembling voice behind her.

"Yes... yes, hear that? Nothing. No more footsteps. He's gone."

Maddie leaned back, adjusting her position, still crouched in the dark, her back to her friend, facing the faint glimmer of light creeping through the opening of the cavern. As her hand grazed the rocky ground, she felt something warm against her fingers.

She frowned, and raised her hand, staring. It was sticky, like sap... warm and slipping down her hand. She blinked a few times, trying to adjust her gaze. And then she risked turning on the light on her phone.

"Battery is almost dead," she whispered. "Can, I use yours?" But Jas didn't reply, and the light from Maddie's phone illuminated red-stained fingers. She went still, blinking in confusion. "Is... Jas are you bleeding?"

"Yes... I'm sorry. I didn't see him coming behind me."

Her friend's voice... but the sentence was longer now. And she picked out the mistakes. A bit too deep towards the end. The cadence wrong. None of the fear that had marked Jasmine's voice in their flight through the snowbound slopes.

A slow prickle of dread crept up her spine now.

"What's the matter, Maddie?" the voice continued. And it was morphing now. Instead of the tone of a young, terrified woman, it changed. Going deeper, more resonant. And then it carried a chuckle. The dark silhouette still leaned there against the wall. Inches from her. The hand still reached out, touching her. The skin warm but no gloves. Why no gloves?

She jolted, turning sharply, trying to absolve her soul of the sudden bout of terror. Her own words died on her lips though. As she whirled and her back struck the stone wall, she coiled like a spring and nearly bolted, but another part of her, a part that was concerned for her friend lingered a split second longer. And as she peered into the cramped space, she realized the shadow behind her was too big. Far too big to be Jas. But that second shadow, off to the side, ten paces back, motionless on the ground?

Bleeding... Her light caught the pool of blood extending from the still form, along the ground towards her.

"Poor Maddie," a distinctly masculine voice whispered in her ear.

And then a hand shot out, snatching at her neck. Her phone illuminated a sleeve, a hand, but nothing more. Maddie was too busy stumbling back. The man missed her by inches. She screamed, kicked. Flung the only thing she had in hand.

Her phone.

It bounced off his face, and he howled in pain.

"That's not nice!" he screeched. His voice a mixture between Jasmine's and his own.

She screamed at him, stumbling struggling, but finally regaining her feet as she kicked and floundered. He lunged after her again, but she spun on her heel and sprinted away, racing out of the tunnel now.

No phone.

Something ripped—the sleeve of her jacket. It tore off in his hand, a blistering cold swelled up her arm where the warm protection had guarded her skin.

But she didn't stop, tripping into the snow, rolling to her feet in a surge of white powder, and racing onward all the same.

"Come back, Maddie!" Jasmine's sweet, soft voice rang out. "Please—please come back!"

She didn't look over her shoulder. She could hear those footsteps thumping along, racing after her. She tried not to scream—she needed the air. Needed her lungs. Needed to *run!*

And so she did, sprinting down the slopes, through the snow, and racing away from the man in hot pursuit.

Alone, helpless...

"No!" she screamed now. But it wasn't so much for the man. Wasn't so much for herself. It was a refusal to the fear.

The terror soaking her bones, creeping down her spine like the steps of some spider. No! No! She refused the fear. Refused to die out in the snow.

Another step. Another, faster...

Miles away from civilization. No car to speak of. No phone to call for help. But she kept the fear at bay at least for another second. And another.

And even when it began to press in, Maddie Porter ran all the same.

CHAPTER 1

"YEAH, ZEKE, I KNOW your daughter is out there." Priscilla Porter snapped, her tongue like a whip as she faced a gray-bearded man in a skullcap. "My cousin is out there, so work *faster* and stop whining!"

Ella watched her sister direct the search parties through the snow from halfway up the mountain, surrounded by prickling firs laden with frost. Behind them, a fleet of emergency vehicles crowded the mountain pass, leading up the thin trail towards where the police, the marshal's service and the sole FBI agent in Nome had gathered.

All hands on deck for this one. The last time Ella had been near her sister, Cilla had tried to shoot through a one-way mirror into an interrogation room. And then she had punched Ella.

They hadn't spoken a word to each other. In fact, neither of them had even met the other's gaze yet. Even though they'd been traipsing through the snow, searching the crime scene for nearly half an hour.

Another search party in orange and bright red uniforms were being sent to the west, once more the group of ten volunteers directed by Cilla.

Ella exhaled slowly, glancing away from where her sister was rallying the third search party, away from the small, ransacked campsite.

An orange tent ripped to shreds. Blood on the snow. Footprints everywhere. An old cooking fire had been doused. The charcoal scattered along the rough ground in spots where snow hadn't managed to cling yet.

Ella glanced at her phone, scrolling quickly through the faces of the seven missing teenagers. All seven from St. Andrew's Academy. An expensive, exclusive, private school—the only one of its type in Nome.

She lingered on the final photo. Susan Thompson. The one who'd planned the trip, gathering some of her friends for an end of semester celebration. The semester schedule for the private school was different than the other schools, ending the first section in October. A week ago.

The trip had been planned for a while. Two young men, five women. And now all of them were missing.

All except for Susan, the trip coordinator.

Ella turned, glancing at the thick tree protruding from the muddy, sloshy ground. Brenner Gunn, her old friend and US marshal, was one of the workers helping to cut the ropes binding Susan to the frozen trunk. The high school senior's arms were pale, stretched back. Her jacket was missing, as well as her shoes. Her toes had turned blue in the snow, and her head lolled lifelessly to the side.

Ella scowled deeply, staring at the body.

"We have cause of death yet?" she called out, her breath turning to feathers of mist.

Brenner Gunn glanced back at her, his scowl dark and deep. The coroner, Dr. Messer, was there. The grandmotherly woman had her trusty compound bow strapped to her back, and she was wearing camo pants. She frowned as she probed at the near-frozen corpse, her ever present smile wrinkles morphing into a steep frown.

"The blow to the back of the head didn't do it," said Dr. Messer. "Nor the cold—it was this laceration here." She pulled down the high collar of the young woman, revealing a deep but narrow cut. "He went for the voice box," said Dr. Messer coolly. "She bled out."

"The voice box?" Brenner asked, wrinkling his nose. His eyes carried an emotion Ella hadn't seen there before. Every time he glanced at the young woman, it was as if he'd seen a ghost. He looked away again, his handsome features creasing into a frown. Though a bit over six foot, he stood hunched now, his shoulders slumped as if in defeat.

Though Brenner had served as a sniper for one of the most elite fighting forces in the world, something about staring at the woman tied to the tree seemed to deflate him.

His eyes carried that haunted sadness often displayed in his solemn blue gaze. Pretty and sad. That was how she saw Brenner. But though he was still limping, favoring his left leg due to an old injury, he looked sober. This was a marked improvement from the previous week when they'd tackled a case on the frozen Bering sea.

Still, he leaned out to brace himself against the nearest tree, loosing a long sigh which carried on the cold.

"See here?" Dr. Messer said, pointing to the neck. "Didn't go for a long slice on the windpipe. Just the voice box." She leaned back, staring up at the mountain peaks, nearly five hundred feet above them. "Gets you wondering, doesn't it?"

"Wondering about what?" Ella asked, approaching slowly, her gloved hands pressed together for additional warmth.

"Oh, you know," said Dr. Messer, the older woman turning to look at Ella. "Stories—the sort of stories my grandbabies enjoy. I'm sure it's nothing."

"Of course it's nothing," said a new voice.

Ella, Brenner and Dr. Messer turned to watch as Priscilla Porter strode towards them. There was something of a sway to the young woman's gait. She had a smug look on her face, but her eyes were pure ice.

"Brenner," Priscilla said, nodding with a smirk towards the ex-SEAL. But the marshal didn't acknowledge her, preferring to stare at the corpse.

Ella nodded politely. She stepped forward to greet her sister. The last time they'd met, Cilla had punched Ella, but Ella had always considered herself the more level-headed of the two. Cilla had never been one to manage her emotions. Cocksure, confident and waspishly smart, Cilla served as the heiress for Porter Enterprises and managed most of the inland mining operations. She was impossible to control, save by one person. Their father, Jameson Porter. Where Jameson was concerned, Cilla had a soft spot and would go to battle no matter the odds. Where anyone else was concerned? Cilla was a tempest to be avoided.

And now that storm was heading towards them. As twins, Ella and Cilla both had the same upturned, celestial noses, porcelain complexions, blonde hair and pretty features, like retired cheerleaders.

Cilla wore small, seashell earrings, a quiet boast in Ella's experience, since Ella was deathly terrified of the ocean and Cilla loved the water.

The two sisters had never seen eye to eye. And until last week, they hadn't seen each other for twelve years. Of course, it wasn't like Cilla hadn't earned the cold shoulder. She *had* kissed Ella's ex-boyfriend after all.

Which, Ella guessed, was why Brenner was refusing to meet Cilla's gaze.

"You're too smart for that sort of thing, Dr. Messer," Priscilla said in a sort of drawl.

Messer smiled back, and to her credit, the expression made it to her eyes. But she did cross her arms, a defensive posture, and turned to face Cilla completely, giving the tempest the full attention she deserved.

"Too smart for what, sweetie?" said the coroner.

"The voice box. These mountains? You're thinking it's the Mocking-bird, right?"

"The what?" Ella asked.

Brenner just snorted. "Bullshit, that's what."

"The Mockingbird is just a story the kids made up a few years ago." Priscilla leaned over, patting Brenner on the arm. "We can both agree on something."

Brenner though knocked her hand away. "Get the hell off me!" he snapped.

Dr. Messer tried to interject, but a voice boomed. "Did you touch my wife, Gunn?"

A man a bit taller than Brenner, but not as handsome, marched to-wards them, away from the nearest search party which was gearing up to head out. His voice echoed with authority. The voice of a man built as a leader of men. He marched forward, shaking his head fiercely. His hands bunched into fists at his sides. "Touch my wife again, and Gunn you're a dead man!"

"Ah, and this is the reason a civilian is organizing the search parties, is it, Ms. Porter?" said Dr. Messer, her tone still peaceable, but carrying an edge. "Hello, Chief Baker."

The broad-shouldered ex-athlete had shaved since the last time Ella had seen him, but stubble had come back and his mustache had grown out. He wore a large, brass belt buckle, and large boots with jeans, giving him the look of a rancher rather than the chief of police. Ella supposed he must have been off hours when he'd gotten the call about Susan Thompson.

Now he strode up to Brenner, scowling. The last time these two had interacted, Brenner had tossed the chief to the floor of the marshal's office. In front of the chief's wife. The bad blood between the four of them went nearly as deep as the crimson staining the snow beneath the tree.

Dr. Messer stepped between them and said, "Biscuit?" There was a crinkling sound of a wrapper, and the older woman produced a small, wax bag which she waved about. Chief Baker snatched one of the pastries, munching on it, crumbs spilling down beneath his mustache.

Ella politely declined. She'd seen where the coroner kept her baked goods the last time she'd been to the morgue.

"What's this Mockingbird?" Ella asked quietly. Her gloved hands tapping with nervous energy against her phone.

Dr. Messer looked to her. "Supposedly a wildman in the mountains. A killer who hunts his victims and steals their voices."

Ella wrinkled her nose. "Steals their voices how?"

"It's said he mimics the victims he takes. Using their voices as his own."

"It's also said he's ten feet tall and can fly," Cilla added dryly. "Just because this girl was stabbed in the voice box doesn't mean—"

"But then there's these tracks!" Messer said. "The ones Mr. Gunn found."

Ella glanced sharply at Brenner. "You found tracks?"

He shrugged sheepishly, extending an arm to point behind the tree. Tattoos were visible just past his wrist, and Ella knew he'd designed some of them himself.

Wanting to frown, but keeping her expression neutral, Ella stepped around the tree, studying the frozen ground. She stared where large footprints led away from the tree. *Very* large. At least two feet across. She leaned down, studying the imprints in the powdery white. Then she straightened, glancing over her shoulder.

"See," Dr. Messer murmured, on edge.

"Snowshoes," Ella replied.

Messer, an accomplished bow-hunter in her own right, scowled. "I know they're *snowshoes*, Ella. But they're large snowshoes."

"Aren't most snowshoes large?"

"Yes... yes, there is that. But it could *also* be used to disguise large feet. There's also that, see!" Messer pointed up with a flourish as if intent on vindication.

The others all turned, glancing towards where a branch, about ten feet in the air, had been snapped.

Priscilla giggled. "You think a ten foot giant accidentally hit his head on that branch? Maybe it's bigfoot."

Messer snapped back, "You're not telling me you don't believe in *bigfoot*?"

Ella, who decided things were starting to derail, cleared her throat hesitantly, stepping forward and staring up at the branch. She said, "I don't... don't know if our killer is ten-feet tall. But I do know that if I wanted to watch a campsite without being seen, I might approach from behind a large tree, scale that tree and stay in the branches until someone passed under me..."

Long ago, Ella had developed an eye for details. And now, she traced scrape marks along the bark, near the shattered branch. Bits of wood torn free, indicating something falling. Then Ella turned, looking up the mountains again. She said softly, "Brenner, do the tracks go any-where?"

"Back about fifteen paces, but once we leave the tree, the wind and snow took the trail."

Ella bit her lip, following the indicating marks. They led further up the mountain.

Chief Baker was murmuring something to his wife now, holding a whispered conference and leaning close so his lips brushed against one of Cilla's seashell ears. Ella caught the words, "Cousin... and father's demand..."

Ella winced briefly.

Brenner sidled up to Ella, his voice warm but thankfully not smelling of alcohol. Dr. Messer returned to examining the body, muttering about, "No bigfoot... fools. Absolute fools."

Brenner whispered. "Who's Maddie Porter to you?"

Ella shifted uncomfortably where she stood so near to Gunn. Twelve years ago, he'd broken up with her. She'd thought she'd seen the last of him, but fate had a funny way of bringing disparate things back into alignment.

Her fingers tapped against the phone in her pocket, feeling the rigid outline through the material. And Brenner wasn't the *only* person from her past she'd never wanted to see again.

Standing so close to the marshal, though, who'd gotten handsomer with age, she found it—if only briefly—difficult to remember *why* she'd left Nome.

She leaned a bit away from him but met his blue eyes with her own pale blue gaze, like the frozen seas. "Maddie's my cousin."

"Shit, I'm sorry. Were you two close?"

"I'm afraid not. She was four the last time I saw her."

"Damn."

Ella ran a hand through her golden hair, brushing it behind an ear and sending another plume of steam from her lips. Priscilla and Chief Baker were inching away from the rest of them, thank God, but still intensely whispering, and Ella didn't like the secrecy or the urgency in their voices.

Brenner distracted her by saying, "Is there... anything you know about Maddie? Do you have her number?"

"No reception up here," Ella said. "I got her number from Baker." More tapping of her fingers against the outline in her pocket. "Maddie is new to Nome, though."

"I thought you said she was here when she was four."

"No. She visited here when she was four. But her father moved her here last year." Ella bit her lip uncomfortably. "He's been very sick for a few years now."

"I get it. Hoping to give Maddie some familiarity with her family before... well..."

"Before he dies, yes. And credit to my mother—whatever else she may be, she's loyal to family. From what Dr. Messer told me, Lois, umm, sorry, *mom,* has been more than welcoming to her brother."

"Wait? Lois' brother? So Maddie is Lois's niece by blood?"

"Yes. What's the... oh, Porter? My father took my mother's name when they married. She is older by a few years."

"Huh. Whatever works."

Ella snorted. "My dad did it for a loophole in the tax code. Nothing is sacred except the almighty ounce of gold. Anyway... I think we should follow that trail."

"Like I said, it vanishes after a few feet."

"Yeah, but it goes back up the slope... Some of the other trails head that way too."

Ella and Brenner both shifted uneasily as they scanned the ruined campsite again. The footsteps went one way then the other. Rapid footsteps with great gaps between them, suggesting the teenagers had fled at a dead sprint.

Susan hadn't been so lucky, but by the looks of things, at least for now, six other teens had managed to escape.

Six teens being hunted in the mountains. Her cousin wasn't the only one up there. She watched as the newest search party moved up the slopes, their bright outfits catching the light. But the light was fading as evening approached. And in the distance, out over the sea, she watched storm clouds being ushered in by saline winds.

A blizzard was predicted by late that night. Time was running out.

"We should hurry," Ella said.

"Want to try the snowmobile?"

Ella hesitated. Chief Baker had expressly forbidden machinery, suggesting the terrain was too treacherous. But what was life without a little risk?

Besides...

Ella found a knot in her gut. The polite greeting to her sister. Over-looking the snide comments and glares. Ella was a rule-follower and tried to stay firmly planted on the straight and narrow. Brenner called her a liar for hiding her emotions more often than not. Ella called it prudent.

But it always came with a cost... A lingering, gnawing sensation that was only ever released through risk and surging adrenaline.

So she nodded firmly. "Snowmobile, yeah... Which one's yours?"

Brenner was turning, though—still refusing to glance at Priscil-la—and limping down the slope with hurried footsteps towards the array of vehicles parked along the narrow, mountain road.

Ella followed quickly. As she did, though, she glanced side to side—determining no one was watching—and surreptitiously pulled her phone from her pocket. Brenner was fiddling with some keys. Messer was examining the body and gesturing towards one of her assistants by the ruined tent to come help take samples. The latest search party moved two at a time up a slope, and Baker was still holding a whispered conference with Cilla, his tone urgent.

But the urgency wasn't the cause of the goosebumps along the back of Ella's arms.

Instead, she stared at the newest text message.

An unknown number.

The same number that had texted her last week. And then had called.

She still remembered that confident, eloquent voice.

The newest text message was from the Graveyard Killer. A notorious murderer with seventeen victims to his name. He left his victims in graveyards on old tombstones.

Once upon a time, Ella had managed to capture the killer. He'd sat in the back of her vehicle, hands cuffed...

Until he'd said something. They'd spoken.

And she'd let him go. On purpose. A secret she was determined to keep to her grave.

But now, the Graveyard Killer was coming to visit. She'd balked at the idea. But the exact words of their exchange was seared into her potent memory. Ella rarely forgot a recollection. She didn't have a photographic memory, but it was close. Another benefit of her attention to detail.

But in her mind she recollected the exchange over the phone.

She'd said, *"You can't come see me. I will arrest you the moment I see you."*

A pause, a deep breath. "A risk I'm willing to take. You're too valuable to my mission. I'll see you soon, Ms. Porter. Have a lovely, sunny day."

She hadn't heard from him in a week.

She'd hoped he'd changed his mind.

But now, there, the three simple letters confirmed her worst fears.

OMW.

On my way.

Shit. She jammed her phone back into her pocket and double-timed to catch up with Brenner's limping form where the tall man arrived at his snowmobile.

One thing at a time. She had to focus on one crisis at a time. The Graveyard Killer was on his way, but another murderer was already in Nome. Hiding in the mountains, hunting six teenagers. Her own cousin.

She scowled, straddling the back of the snowmobile as it grumbled to life. A blizzard was coming in over the seas. A killer was coming to visit Ella. But a monster hunted the mountains, and it was up to her to focus, to push aside distraction, and to catch the murderer and rescue the other would-be victims.

"Go fast," she whispered in Brenner's ear.

She caught a glimpse of his smirk as he affixed his ski mask.

"You got it," he muttered.

Then he gunned the engine.

CHAPTER 2

She'd treated him like a common criminal, and he'd vowed his revenge.

Jameson Porter puffed slowly on a cigar, standing in the parlor and peering out at the mountains, his expression creased into a frown. He let the smoke billow through the cracked window, standing tall. With sharp features, clean-cut, his silver hair neatly arranged, the patriarch of Porter Enterprises looked every bit the prestige and power he intended to communicate.

A cigar in one hand, his phone was gripped in the other.

"Yes, tonight," Jameson said quietly. "I'm sure. I'll pay triple if you want. Just get it done."

He frowned, lowering his cigar and tapping it against the windowsill, allowing a small pile of ash to form on the ledge, which the wind from the mountains swept against the sill.

"Why?" he said slowly, listening to the voice on the other line. "Do I need a why? You've never asked why before—just take the job." He felt a sudden surge of rage. "I *know* she's my daughter, imbecile. Do you want the job or not?"

He listened as the voice on the other line weighed their options. Normally, this particular contractor could be trusted to accomplish even the most difficult assignments. But Jameson felt a wave of unease as he stared out his parlor window. The mansion was empty now. Lois was still in physical therapy after the incident the previous week. His wife had been shot.

Jameson had been prevented from taking matters into his own hands because he'd been in an interrogation room, hands cuffed.

He didn't care that Eleanor was his daughter. She'd crossed a line, and Jameson *kept* his word. And his grudges.

"Scare her, yes… Let her know why." He listened. "I'm sure. As in *dead* dead. No, I won't change my mind. Just do it. Don't call until it's finished."

He hung up, his hand shaking, lowering the phone.

Jameson's eyes flashed in the glass. His features weren't the sort of handsome someone swiped right on. They were a refined sort of beauty. Sharp angles and steep jawline. Handsome in the sort of way that belonged on a movie poster or a political ad. His fingers tapped against his leg where his revolver jutted from a concealed holster attached to his belt over his hip.

No imprinting, either. A sleekly designed revolver holster of seamed leather. The same revolver his grandfather had once used to kill a charging black bear in those very mountains.

He pulled the weapon from his hip, moving fast. Holstered it again. Pulled once more, frowning. It kept catching on the hem of his pants. He scowled now, turning away from the window, glancing down at his weapon.

Brenner Gunn, back at the marshal's office, had been so quick on the draw, Jameson had nearly missed it.

He hesitated, then raised his phone again, texting. *Watch out for the marshal. He's quick.*

This done, he took the small burner phone, pushed open the glass door leading from the parlor onto the porch and tossed the device into the small, metal bin. He snatched the lighter fluid from the wooden shelf where he kept incidentals and poured it in the can.

Then he tossed the stub of his cigar in as well. A *whoosh* as the gas erupted, and flames licked the rim of the container.

He stared, mesmerized as the flame had its way, searing the cheap plastic and turning it into a hunk of nothing.

The phone couldn't be traced back to him. One of his miners had purchased it with cash. The call wouldn't be traced either. His contact was a consummate professional.

"Six…" he said, chuckling. "Sixth time's the charm?"

He'd hired this particular frontiersman five times already. Five contracts, five bodies—not a whiff of a cop. It helped that his son-in-law was the Chief of Police. But still...

Priscilla also played interference.

If only *both* his daughters were so loyal.

He watched the phone burn a bit longer then turned, shutting the door behind him, the cold air swirling in after him. He stepped into the house, pausing to glance at one of the framed photos over the expansive, marble mantelpiece.

Most of the photos were of the three of them. Lois, Jameson and Priscilla. A couple were of his brother-in-law, Mark, and of Mark's daughter Maddie. But one photo in particular sat on the mantlepiece. A picture of the *four* of them. His wife, himself, the twins...

Ella was only a teenager in that photo. He stared at it, feeling a faint lump in his throat. He reached up, rubbing at his face, blinking a few times.

Then he snatched the photo with a snarl, shoved open the door to the patio and tossed the photo in the burning can.

"To hell with you," he muttered beneath his breath.

He paused again, inhaling the scent of ash, the nip of the frigid air. He adjusted his sleeves, smoothed back an errant curl tossed on his forehead, and then breathed slowly. The mist of breath matched the usual plume of cigar smoke.

He stared at the mountains again.

Ella had crossed him. Had humiliated him. He'd vowed his vengeance, and sentimentality would only get in the way.

A king didn't build a kingdom by allowing offense to go unpunished, no matter *who* it came from. He'd given her a chance. He'd tried—he really had.

But now…

The call had been made. The die cast.

The hitman was on his way.

***

The frontiersman lowered the phone, wrinkling his nose and staring. He spat off to the side, black tobacco staining the snow. He watched from the assembly of volunteers as his target mounted the back of a snowmobile, her hands latching onto the black, rigid handles under the jutting seat.

His phone buzzed again, and he glanced down. *Watch out for the marshal. He's quick.*

The frontiersman frowned, glancing at the second figure on the front of the snowmobile. Brenner Gunn. He'd known Brenner—grown up with Brenner. Hell, he'd even known Ella back in the day. Nome, born and bred. His father a crab fisherman, his mother... well, known for crabs of another variety. The whore. He smirked at his own joke. "Funny," he said to himself. He often talked to himself. He found it soothing.

A contract was a contract.

He hadn't failed one yet.

"Damn good pay," he said again. A passing volunteer hesitated. "Umm, sorry?"

The frontiersman shook his head. "Not talkin' to you."

"Oh. Oh, sorry." The nervous volunteer hastened up the slope to join the others, waving at where Chief Baker and Priscilla Porter were in hushed conversation.

The frontiersman adjusted his own pistol on his hip, tested the knife at his belt. He smiled faintly as gloved fingers trailed along the marks cut into the hilt. Each mark a memory. Each one more precious than the last. He always remembered the light leaving their eyes. Their last breath.

Eleanor Porter would be no different. And if he could bag a bear like Mr. Gunn along the way? It would only help pad his resume.

Brenner wasn't the only man in Alaska with special forces training. SEALs were well-known among the lower forty-eight. But Green Berets?

"Damn SEALs," he said. He liked the sound of his own voice. Liked the sound of *any* voice really. Two years in solitary confinement had a way of shaping one's predilections.

The frontiersman adjusted his gloves, straddled his own snowmobile, and began to pull from behind his truck, where he'd hauled the thing up the mountain. Army vs. Navy. A debate as old as time. SEAL vs Green Beret.

Brenner had only served five years, though.

The frontiersman had served ten.

Brenner had been a sniper but the frontiersman had made a name for himself up close and personal.

Five kills so far in civvy life.

But over there? In the dunes and the hot sand? Fifty. More.

Sand, snow... what was the difference? Both stained red just as easy.

He gunned his snowmobile, lowered his head, and—keeping his distance—followed Brenner and Ella up the mountain.

CHAPTER 3

ELLA STARED UP THE slopes, wincing against the glare of the sunlight off the ice. The reflection was blinding. A pristine, undisturbed landscape claimed her attention.

"See anything?" she said, leaning in, pressing against Brenner's back.

He fidgeted at the proximity, and she leaned back just as quickly. Brenner threw his bad leg over the edge of the snowmobile, tilting his head back and letting out a long, fogging breath. He watched as the wind carried the steam one way. Then he looked at the ground. "Wind changed an hour ago," he said with a nod.

The snowmobile rested on a rocky outcrop near the top of a mountain trail laden with packed ice. The two of them dismounted, both of them faced with the grim reality of having to hoof it if they wanted to go further.

Ella shot a look over her shoulder, down the trail—she'd lost sign of the search party. Earlier, she'd seen a man on a snowmobile moving slowly up the slopes. But he was gone now, too.

The wind seemed louder up here, undeterred, and it whistled and whined as it swept the cliffs in a constant pattern, disturbing the top layer of fresh snow, concealing tracks, obscuring patterns in the ice.

"Wish we hadn't had fresh fall last night," Brenner said scowling. His voice matched their surroundings. A cold voice. A distant voice.

Ella considered their options. She leaned back on the snowmobile, supported by engine-warmed metal paneling. "We can keep going... or..."

"Or what?"

"Maybe we took a wrong turn..." Ella frowned, wincing against the glare off the snow, her eyes tracing one way then another. "I'm not a tracker," she said.

"Neither am I. Not really."

"I thought marshals were known for finding fugitives."

"Yeah, well... hell. I'm not *awful,* but I'm no big game hunter."

Ella winced. Big game. Nome and its surroundings were known for other monsters—not just killers. Bears, wolves lurked these snow-bound cliffs.

"What's up here?" Ella said. "This is the Callaway pass, right? Which means that peak over there..." she pointed off to the east, about a mile away. "Is that where the old off-grid commune still is?"

Brenner shrugged. "Think so. They keep to themselves, though. Doubt they did this."

"Right... right, but... If any of the kids were looking for refuge, somewhere to hide?"

"Yeah... I mean, could be worth checking with the off-gridders. But... you know, something about those tracks down there."

"Snowshoes."

"Right. Ground was packed leading *up* the trail. So if he followed them from town..."

"Why the snowshoes."

"Yeah, and the trail disappeared, but it *did* point this way."

Ella turned again, looking further up towards the peak, breathing in shallow puffs. About three hundred feet of towering rock on her horizon, like a giant tidal wave frozen in space. "So you think maybe he has a place up there? Damn... wish I'd thought to request a drone."

"Baker has a couple back in a truck. We could go and ask him..."

Ella snorted. "Which of us do you think he dislikes least?"

"I mean... I'm the one who hit him."

"Yeah, but his wife has hated me for two decades."

"Fair. Well... So we either check out the off-gridders commune. We go back get some drones. Or we keep going and see if we can find some shelter. Maybe one of the kids. Or, damn... I dunno, a homebuilt killer cabin."

"Killer cabin. Nice." Ella shivered. It wasn't in her nature to back down from a challenge. Besides, even with drones, they'd have to ascend the cliffs again. She dusted snow off her gloves, looking at Brenner. "Do we know anything about Susan Thompson?"

"What do you mean?"

"I mean... was she well-liked among her peers?"

Brenner stared at her. "Shit. You think the kids mighta done this? Killed her and ran? Made it look like something it isn't..."

"It's possible. We weren't there."

Brenner winced, shaking his head. "I hate this."

"Me too."

"No, like I really... really hate this. It's in my chest, Ella. It's glass in my chest."

She hesitated at this characterization, studying his cold, sad eyes. "How long... since you've had... well..."

"Damn it. This isn't about drinking. Okay. It's... youngsters. Kids. I... I swear, Ella, if I found who did this, I'll put them in the snow. I swear I will."

"I'll have to stop you if you try," she admonished. But her heart wasn't in it.

"And a week."

"What?"

"Sober a week—that's what you were asking, right? Whatever. So what's the call, Agent Porter?"

She smirked. "Weird to hear you call me that." Her fingers tapped against the outline of the phone in her pocket. The further they went, the worse the reception was. In a way, it was a boon. *On my way.*

"Let's go a bit further. If we find nothing, we can go get those drones."

"Roger. Have to hoof it from here. Too thick. Snowshoes are in the black bag."

Ella reached out, snagging the indicated baggage item and unzipping it with shivering fingers as she reached for the snowshoes.

The blizzard was still coming in fast. She could see it, miles away, darkening the sky. The longer they took, the more dangerous it would become. There were six teenagers still missing, hiding or... worse.

She scowled now, her dark features matching the persuasion of the skyline. With quick motions, she bent and began to attach the snow-shoes.

As she did, Brenner said. "Hey... actually, I think there's a spot a few minutes that way... Some old caverns and connecting tunnels. Might be worth checking out but..." He hesitated, frowning. "If we get caught up there in the blizzard, it'll be hell."

Ella didn't hesitate. "I'm not worried."

"Neither am I," he said defensively. "Just... maybe if we wait until the storm passes..."

Ella shook her head, though, determinedly. "No waiting. We don't have the luxury."

Brenner sighed, looking like he might add more, but then he shrugged, nodded and pointed and began to trudge towards the caves.

CHAPTER 4

Maddie Porter stumbled through the snow, gasping now.

"Don't stop. Don't stop. Don't stop." This chant was her version of the Little Engine That Could. Her eyes fixated on the small, wooden structure she'd spotted through the terrain. Rough, scabby trees jutted from the road on either side, like sentries flanking the way in consummate welcome.

The small, log cabin had splintered beams jutting from beneath a rough-hewn roof support. Thick, naked beams of wood sat on top of each other. Maddie didn't know much about Nome, but her father had made her read books on the town, and Alaska in general, the week before they'd come to this place.

And she vaguely recognized the style of the old, wooden home with the hallmarks of Swedish craftsmanship. The pictures in her mind—she'd always had a good memory, just like her Uncle Jameson—matched some of the way the logs settled on each other. Small glimpses of moss and detritus was visible as insulation, dripping down from places under the logs.

She stumbled towards the building, moving in soaked boots—she could no longer feel her toes. Another thing she knew, and this she hadn't needed the book for, was the threat of hypothermia and frostbite. She needed fire. Needed to warm herself.

"Hello!" she called out, waving a hand towards the cabin. "Hello—please! Help me!"

But no response. The small, wooden structure sat desolate and abandoned against the side of the mountain.

She shot a look over her shoulder. That horrible figure was long gone. She'd lost him in the tunnels. The tunnels where Jasmine's body lay on the ground, dead... dead... dead...

She sobbed, her voice shaking, but then bit her lip, allowing the pain to help her focus. "No," she snapped at herself. "Don't stop. Don't stop." She reached the front of the small, wooden cabin, her feet *thumping* against the stairs.

She let out a shaking, rattling sigh of air, closing her eyes and feeling moisture from condensation against her eyelashes.

Maddie shot a look over her shoulder, scanning the distant, stunted tree line. Her shoulders were shaking under her jacket, her gloved fingers trembling at her side as she dripped and scattered snow onto the wooden deck of the small house.

An old, splintered chair settled under a dusty window.

The door was half open, with deep gouge marks in the wood. She stared, wide-eyed, exhaling slowly.

"H-hello?" she said tentatively. But then she thought better of it and sealed her lips. Instead, she took a tentative step forward, her motions wobbly now. The momentum alone had been carrying her forward, and now her legs threatened to give out from under her.

She collapsed against the windowsill, holding her breath as if in anticipation. She peered through the glass, fogging the dusty window. Inside, the sparse cabin had been ransacked. Not too dissimilar to the camp back down the mountain.

She shivered, trembling, remembering the horror from the previous night. Or was it two nights ago?

She shook her head, trying to focus. Inside, small pieces of wooden furniture had been shattered. A table turned to kindling. A single curtain over a spartan counter had been ripped, deep furrows gouged in the fabric as if from knives...

The man in the mountains—the one who'd killed Jasmine, the one pursuing her—wasn't alone. He had something else that traveled with him. A monster... A real, honest-to-goodness monster like she'd never seen before.

It had been dark. She hadn't gotten a good look at it, but then again, she hadn't wanted to. They'd all been screaming. All of them running.

At first, she'd thought it was some demon, rising from near the campfire, slobbering and growling. Teeth the size of fingers. But it had been pale, like a ghost. And... she hadn't seen much else. Because like the others, as the tent had ripped, she'd turned to flee.

And that's when she'd heard Susan's voice. Yelling out at them. "Let's play, my new friends! Let's play a game!" Then the cackling laugh. Still in Susan's voice, but *not* Susan. No... something far worse.

It didn't make sense. Maddie was *not* a superstitious person. At least... she hadn't been. But how could she explain everything she'd seen? Ghosts weren't real. Demons weren't either, were they?

But the stories her friends had whispered. The Mockingbird. A monster that lurked in these mountains.

Half wildman.

But half... something else.

And when he changed, under the moon, he hunted his prey, and mimicked their voices to lure unwitting hikers. She hadn't believed the ghost stories. Terry had been particularly interested in telling her all about the horrible tales.

Then again, Terry had developed a crush on her. The large seventeen-year-old was a bit too odd for her, though. Far too fascinated with creepy, dangerous things. Almost as if... she remembered Terry by the campfire, telling a grisly campfire tale...

It had been as if Terry had *enjoyed* their fear. Especially the girls. He'd liked hearing them squeal in fright and horror. Had even laughed when Susan had yelled at him to stop.

She shivered. Monster or not, she hoped she didn't stumble into Terry up here. Especially not alone.

For now, though the cabin had been ransacked at some prior date, it was unoccupied.

Temporary shelter. She could build a fire, warm her feet, and then move again.

She had to keep moving. A blizzard was coming—they'd all been warned about the storm before leaving. Told—no, *required* by their parents to promise they'd come in a full day before the blizzard hit.

That had been the plan.

Then everything had gone to hell...

Maddie shivered, pushed into the ransacked cabin, closing the door behind her. A sudden *creak.* A sudden yelp from the corner.

She yelled, spinning sharply, eyes wide. A figure was crouched in the corner—a small, hunched, dark figure. And the moment Maddie stepped into the cabin, the figure screamed, something flashing metal as the silhouette surged at her with an inhuman howl.

CHAPTER 5

"BLOOD THERE, BRENNER, CAREFUL," Ella murmured pointing at the ground. She winced, crouched now, staring towards the trail of slick red across the stony terrain.

Brenner cursed. "Look—dammit. A body! Hey! Hey, you! Are you okay?"

Ella reached the body in the tunnel ahead of Brenner. A young woman, the same age as Susan, most likely. Stiff and motionless, her unblinking, lifeless gaze staring up at the ceiling in a wide-eyed expression of permanent fear.

Ella cursed, glancing back over her shoulder, towards the mouth of the tunnel. She fumbled her phone, pulling it out and checking through the faces. "Jasmine Swallow," she whispered, her voice trembling. "God dammit. It's another one... SAT phone still have charge?"

Brenner was already fumbling with the emergency communication device, pulling it from his belt. As he did, his shirt lifted, revealing the holster to his handgun. Ella hated to admit it, but having Brenner with her—especially an *armed* Brenner—she felt a surge of security.

Brenner lifted the phone, checked, and then made the call.

No one answered.

"Dammit, Baker, don't be an ass," snapped Brenner. He tried again. And finally, on the sixth ring, a response.

"What the hell do you want, Gunn?" Baker's thick voice snapped. "I'm busy."

"Yeah? Well, we found another kid."

A pause. The tone lightened. "Alive?"

"No. Jasmine Swallow. She's in the old tunnels. Remember them? The ones where you used to take Margaret when you two wanted to avoid her parents knowing what—"

A quick cough and a curse. "Yeah, I know the tunnels, Gunn. Swallow—you're sure she's dead?"

Brenner dropped to the ground, touching at the woman's frigid skin. Ella's glove was off, and she—with some futility—pressed her fingers against the young woman's neck but of course there was no pulse.

Brenner's eyes flashed with that same pain she'd seen before. A haunted sort of look. He kept the phone raised. "I'm sending coordinates. Get the coroner up here. Might need those drones too."

"Roger. That it?"

"No, hang on. Umm... did we... did any of the search parties find anyone?"

"We've got one, yeah," Baker said. "Alive."

It might have been Ella's imagination, but the way Baker said that last word almost felt as if he were boasting. As in, we found *ours* alive.

"Who?" Ella asked, rising to her feet, and putting her glove back on.

"Terry Havek. We found him halfway to the old off-grid commune. Know those guys?"

"Yeah," Ella said quickly. "Can we speak to Terry?"

"I guess. He'll be here for another hour while we clear some of the vehicles—morons blocked the path. But you better hurry. I'm not keeping him here for you."

"Understood," Ella replied.

Brenner lowered the SAT phone and the line went dead. He frowned at her. "Coulda pulled rank. You know—use the bureau to *make* him keep Terry until we spoke to him."

Ella shook her head. "More flies with honey."

"Psh. That's a myth."

Ella shook her head grimly, staring at the body on the ground. "Well... around these parts, I've been hearing that myths are a bit more substantive. Do we just... wait and leave her?"

Brenner cursed, rubbing the back of his head. "I mean... say... look there."

Ella did, following his pointed finger. She spotted it. A footprint in the blood, near the cavern wall. A small print—a small shoe.

"Think one of the other kids was here?" Ella asked, staring and feeling a spike of hope. "She might still be alive."

"Yeah... I think that there—see it, near the rock. That's another print, but nothing after. Not gonna find her that way. You don't think..." Brenner winced. "You don't think maybe this other girl killed Jasmine, do you?"

Ella shook her head. "I won't rule anything out." She was stooped again, going through the victim's pockets. The wound to the woman's throat matched the one on Susan Thompson. Jasmine's coat was missing as well. Her shoes gone too. Same as Susan.

Strange... who was stealing coats and jackets? It was the act of a sadist who wanted to prevent his victims from fleeing in the snow... but why *kill* and *then* take? Unless he'd first taken their shoes, terrorized them, then killed them...

"What are you thinking?" Brenner asked.

"Nothing nice," Ella replied with a heavy sigh. She shook her head, then said. "You know what... one second. Here—give me your flashlight."

"Right on, boss."

Ella took the light, pointing it in the back of the cavern. The small tunnel ended in a sort of dry cave. Ella approached the dusty, stone wall, studying it, frowning as she did. "Something look off to you about this?" she murmured.

Brenner stared at the wall and then, in response, he pushed.

The stone gave way... except it wasn't stone at all. But rather a light material of wood and foam, painted to blend with the gray walls.

Brenner hadn't anticipated the give, and so he yelped as he stumbled forward. Another, larger tunnel led through this hidden door, curling around.

"Holy crap," Brenner said. "Looks like this thing curves around, yeah? Maybe back out further up?"

"Let's check. But quick. I still want to speak to the survivor."

"At least we have one," Brenner said, his voice shaking. "One for the good guys."

"Yeah... here, point your light there... No, never mind, just moss... It must be warmer in here. Strange."

Brenner and Ella moved along this hidden tunnel, but didn't have far to go. Like Brenner had guessed, the tunnel curved and deposited them on a small precipice fifteen feet above the initial tunnel entrance where they'd found Jasmine's body. Ella and Brenner stepped out onto the small rocky outcrop, peering down towards their footprints in the snow below.

"Hey!" Ella said sharply. "Look—look here!" She stepped forward towards a scrubby, tangled plant. This, she guessed, was where the killer must have climbed to creep in behind the girl in the tunnel. Girls? Ella still wasn't sure how to explain the bloody footprint.

But this? She reached out, snagging a piece of fabric from the plant, raising it for Brenner to see.

"Look at this," she murmured.

"Strange... Periwinkle. Not a very common color."

"Not at all," Ella said, her voice shaking. "It's from one of their school uniforms."

"What?"

"It's the same color as St. Andrew's Academy's uniforms."

"No... No Susan's was darker than that."

Ella turned to Brenner, fumbling for her phone, pulling it out and scrolling through the victim images. She didn't forget details. And these were seared into her mind. She raised *two* of the pictures. The two boys. Terry Havek and James Bender. Terry was a senior, but almost twenty years old. He'd started school late and had been held back a year. James Bender was an athlete, and according to Zeke Chernow—the man who Cilla had been tongue-lashing on the search teams—had been dating his daughter Carrie. Another one of the missing kids.

Brenner scowled at the two photos, raising the piece of periwinkle fabric and touching it with gloved fingers against the screen, up near the boys' uniforms.

"A match," Ella said slowly. "The girls' uniforms are darker than the boys'. This is a match. A perfect match."

Brenner scowled, lowering the fabric, and turning. "We should go speak with Terry Havek."

***

Ella dismounted the snowmobile, not waiting for Brenner to follow. She hastened towards the small gathering of police officers by a waiting SUV. Other vehicles were still being shuffled further down the road, kicking up clouds of ice and snow.

Ella moved towards them, hands in her pockets, head ducked. She hated that they'd been forced to leave Jasmine's body back on the mountain. But they'd done their best to use snow to blockade the entrance to the tunnel, to prevent any creature from sneaking in and desecrating the body.

On a more practical level, Ella also didn't want her crime scene disturbed.

But a witness had lived. The oldest one of the friend group. And it so happened that a piece of fabric perfectly matching his school uniform had been found near the brush that led to a secret entrance which the killer must have used to sneak up behind Jasmine Swallow.

Ella marched down the trail, moving along a steel guard rail protecting her from a sharp plummet towards jutting rocks far below.

Her eyes were fixated on the cops by the SUV, and also seeking out the large figure sitting in the front seat, visible through the glass.

She almost didn't notice the movement off to the left. A silhouette emerging from behind a tree. To the right, the guard rail protected a steep fall. To the left, the steep ground found a sharp incline and created a hill overlooking the vehicles.

And there, behind a large fir with a wide trunk, she spotted a figure step out. She only had a split second to notice the man's gun.

Pointed straight at her.

Her heart leapt, but she didn't have time to think. Didn't have time to yell. She watched him tense, watched as he prepared to fire.

There was no cover in front, no cover behind. Only the guard rail and the open trail.

And so, heart in her throat, her lungs stoppered in a surge of fear, Ella did the only thing she could think. She leapt the guardrail, over the precipice.

And then a loud *bang! Bang!* Bullets sparked off the metal rail as she plummeted, missing her by inches.

CHAPTER 6

MADDIE PORTER FAILED TO hold back her scream as the hunched figure lunged towards her with a howl. A glimpse of wide, gaping eyes filled with terror. A small butter knife clutched in one hand—the same knife they'd used to pare back smore sticks—with varying degrees of success, thanks to the blunt tool.

"Carrie!" Maddie yelled, stumbling back. "Carrie it's me!" She felt a sudden surge of relief, staring at her friend. The other teenage girl froze, blinking back. "Maddie? Maddie, oh thank God! I thought you were him!"

Her friend's hand lowered slowly, still gripping the butter knife tightly. She didn't lower it completely though, shaking horribly.

"Carrie..." Maddie said tentatively. "It's *me*..."

Carrie glanced past her nervously, towards the door, then back again. "Were you the one who helped him? Huh?" A note of panic in her voice. The accusation carried by the demand.

"Was I the one who... what?"

Carrie shook her head though, the butter-knife lifting slowly. "Was it you, Maddie! Tell me!"

"Keep your voice down," Maddie whispered fiercely. "He's still out there. He killed Jasmine."

Carrie gaped, her mouth unhinged. "Oh... Oh God... Jas is dead?"

"Yes! Now shush."

But Carrie's knife leapt up again. As her eyes darted to the door, they finally settled on Maddie, wide as hubcaps. "No!" she screamed. "No, no! I heard it—it must have been you. You're the one who left the tent! I saw you."

Maddie just stared, trying to make sense of this. She held her hands up slowly. She wasn't *too* frightened of the butter knife. Maddie had grown up as an athlete. A swimmer and a soccer star. If it came to a fight, she thought her chances of disarming the terrified girl were high.

Carrie was wearing her school sweater, the dark red hue—Maddie realized grimly—would perfectly hide any blood. Her jacket was unzipped, though, suggesting Carrie had been hiding in the small, wooden building long enough not to feel the chill as much. There was evidence of coals in the corner. A small fire made from splinters and broken furniture. The fire was cold now.

"Have you been here all night?" Maddie whispered.

"Wouldn't you like to know!" Carrie snapped. "Don't lie to me, Maddie. I saw you leave the tent!"

"Yes! I'm sorry, I didn't realize I had to have a two-day bladder."

"No—no, I heard him talking to you!"

Maddie frowned. "What?"

"Yes! Don't deny it!"

"No one was talking to me!"

"They were! I *heard* him."

"Carrie, you're not making any sense. Look, my hands are up. I have no weapon. He's not here. Just tell me what you mean. You heard the monster talking to someone?"

"There's no such thing as monsters!" snapped Carrie.

Maddie snorted. "You saw that thing. It ripped the tent to shreds."

"It was a wolf."

"Too big for a wolf, Carrie."

"Well, I don't know what it was. But he was whistling at it. It was listening to *him*!"

So Maddie had been right. She'd heard the same thing but hadn't believed it. The killer—the crazed wildman had disappeared. And then the monster had shown up. Had he been *whistling* to control it?

Or had he transformed into it? Like the stories Terry had told them. A man who could take the form of a demon-wolf. A monster in the night... The Mockingbird didn't just take his victims' voices, he used it to hunt his prey. According to Terry's stories, the monster *never* stopped hunting once it set its sight on someone.

Maddie shot a quick look through the dusty window.

The trail outside the cabin was empty. She looked back at Carrie.

Her friend had lowered the knife again, but was shaking horribly, sobbing. "I... I heard him say, *thank you. Thank you for bringing them here.* He asked who to kill first, and I heard the name Susan... I think it was your voice!"

"No way!" Maddie yelled. "You didn't hear my voice. Impossible!"

"It had to be you. All the others were in the tent with me! I counted them!"

Ella stared, blinking. "What... what about the boys' tent?" she demanded.

"What?"

"So let's say I was missing from the girls' tent. Because I had to answer nature's call. What if one of the boys was helping?"

"So you admit it! You know someone was helping him!"

"That's what you're saying! I'm just believing you."

"I'm not making it up! I heard him. From above. I know how it sounds, Maddie—don't look at me like that. But he was above... I think he was in the tree. And he was talking to someone."

"What if he was just mimicking them?"

"I thought so... but I looked outside the tent. I saw another person. Someone at the base of the tree, looking up. I think... I think it was you, Maddie! It looked like you!"

"No it didn't. How could it have. It wasn't me!"

"Someone was helping him. I think they brought us *to* him on purpose!"

"Susan planned the trip. Not me."

"Yes, but Susan wanted to camp by the off-gridders. She thought it would be safer."

"Well... Who's idea was the mountain spot, then?"

"Terry... No, no wait it was James."

Maddie frowned. "I think you're right. I think it was Terry."

"It was one of the boys."

"That's what I'm saying!" Maddie insisted, shivering horribly and pressing her teeth so they wouldn't chatter. "One of the boys from their tent must have gone to speak with him. But... but if that's true." She grimaced. "That's horrible! Terry or James helped the monster find us!"

"There's no such thing as monsters!"

"Yes, there is!"

"No, there isn't!

"Yes, there... Carrie..."

"What?"

"D-do you hear that?"

"Stop it, Maddie. That's not funny."

"No, Carrie. I'm serious. It's... it's on the roof!"

The two girls froze in place, both staring up, listening.

Thump. Thump. Thump.

Footsteps on the roof. Someone moving from the back of the ceiling towards the middle. A pause. The roof groaned slowly, protesting the weight.

"Carrie... Carrie," Maddie whispered desperately. "We have to go. Come on—come on!"

"No! I'm not leaving."

"Carrie, *now!*"

"No!"

Maddie shook her head in horror, staring up at the center of the ceiling. She tried to snatch at her friend's arm. Tried to pull her back. But Carrie slashed at her with the butter knife, the dull metal stinging her palm through her glove.

"Carrie—run!" Maddie snapped, her voice fierce.

But her friend was sobbing, standing, staring up. She'd found protection in this cabin. The four walls, the roof, it had served as her source of comfort. But now, that comfort threatened? It was like ripping away a security blanket.

And in that faltering hesitation, Carrie made the wrong choice, and there was nothing Maddie could do.

She swallowed, glancing out the window. Something was in the snow... something large. Very large—and certainly inhuman. Something was on the roof.

Had someone helped the killer?

One of the boys?

Was Carrie lying or mad or telling the truth?

Thump. Thump.

And then the wood on the ceiling shattered. In a stream of splinters and broken, moldered beams, a shadow fell through the roof, landing on top of Carrie.

Maddie screamed, but instead of going out the front door, towards where she'd spotted the dark shadow, she sprinted towards the window above the spartan sink. She grabbed a chair—one of its legs missing—flung it. The glass shattered.

She heard a scream behind her. Laughter.

"Bye, Maddie!" said Carrie's voice. "I'm going to miss you, Maddie! See you soon." A pleasant, high pitched, sweet voice. A playful, lyrical sound to the voice.

The scream though had also been Carrie's.

Maddie didn't look back. She scrambled over the counter, avoiding the glass, desperate. "Don't stop. Don't stop."

Breathing heavily, terror in her bones, she slipped through the window. Something touched at her ankle as she did, and she screamed in revulsion, stumbling in the snow.

But fear was fuel. Fear would help her forward. *Don't stop. Don't stop.*

She sprinted forward now, away from the cabin, listening as laughter chased her through the mountains.

CHAPTER 7

Brenner heard the gunshots before he spotted the sparks off the guard rail. His stomach plummeted as Ella dove over the metal barrier, off the precipice.

Gunn cursed, breaking into a dead sprint, as shouts erupted. Cops, near an SUV, reached for their weapons, desperately looking for the source of the gunshots.

Brenner spotted the figure instantly. Moving behind the trees, hastening away.

Gunn raised his weapon in a heartbeat, squeezing off two shoots. The rapid motion came as instinctual as drawing breath. One moment he'd been motionless, parking his snowmobile, the next he'd spun on his heel, broken into a sprint while simultaneously drawing his weapon and squeezing off return fire.

Memories of a past life, another country, another mission surfaced.

He heard a curse, a grunt. The figure in the trees stumbled, but kept going.

Brenner snarled. He'd hit the bastard, but not dead center. Too much movement, the tree-line too thick. Too distracted by—

"Ella!" he yelled, turning completely away from the gunman in the trees, holstering his weapon as quickly as he'd drawn it and throwing himself to the edge of the railing.

He stared down, panicked. No sign of her. No sign of—

"Little help," she groaned, her voice carried by a burst of air.

She was hanging onto the metal, two feet to his left. He let out a gasp of relief and reached out, trying to snag her hand. His chest pressed against the metal barrier, scraping over the punctures from the bullets.

Her fingers were taut, whitened at the knuckles where she hung onto a strained metal ridge. Her legs dangled below her, kicking at stone and sending pebbles scampering down the side of the precipice. It took a full five seconds before one of the falling pebbles made tapping sounds, like hailstones, against the sharp rocks below.

Brenner grabbed at Ella's wrist, pulling with his full might.

A hand snaked past him, and Brenner flinched. But Chief Baker leaned over as well, grabbing Ella's other hand. "Heave, man!" Baker yelled. "Heave!"

Brenner had been doing just this, and so he continued to do so.

The two of them pulled Ella back over the railing, onto the road. She didn't topple, didn't hit her knees. But rather, as if she'd simply been ushered through someone's front door, she stood straight, adjusted her jacket and nodded at each of them. "Thank you," she said.

Nothing in her voice communicated fear. Nothing in her eyes suggested terror. Nothing in her posture implied she'd nearly been shot or smashed to pieces.

A simple nod. A simple thank you. And then, as if absolutely nothing had happened, Ella began marching back towards the car where Terry Havek was being kept.

"Hey, hey hold on!" Brenner said, hand on his weapon again, eyeing the slopes.

Three other police were stepping up the incline, moving hastily, their own guns drawn. Chief Baker was now speaking rapidly into a shoulder mic. "Attention, attention search parties. Return to base. I repeat, return to base. We have a live shooter. Come back—now! All units respond to the following coordinates..."

As Baker continued, Brenner stepped between Ella and the slope where he'd spotted the gunman. "Are you okay?" he demanded.

Ella glanced at him. No one else would have noticed it. In his opinion, this was because no one else knew Ella Porter nearly as well as he did.

But there was a glimmer of fear in her eyes. She masked it with a quick nod. "I'm fine."

"Someone just shot at you!" Brenner yelled at her, snatching her wrist now and pulling sharply.

She spun to face him, looking down at her wrist, then up at him. "Let go," she said quietly.

Even now, she didn't lose her temper. Brenner wasn't sure the last time he'd truly seen her let loose. But reluctantly, he released his grip. He pointed at her. "You need to get in your car and head back to town."

"What? No."

"You nearly died and you're acting like you're on a stroll!"

Ella adjusted her sleeves again. Parts of her gloves were ripped, and when she spotted this, she lowered her hands.

She considered his words, and then, in an even tone, her voice only *barely* shaking, she said, "I know. They're looking for him. But I have a mission here, Brenner. We need to talk to Terry. The fabric from *his* school uniform was found near the—"

"No, hang on. It wasn't his uniform. It just was the same color. We don't know if—"

"Right. No, you're right. I'm sorry."

"God damn, don't apologize to me. Stop it. Please—get in your car. Okay?"

Ella shook her head. "I can't do that. There are kids out there, Brenner." And then she turned away from him. It was like watching a sleepwalker. They communicated, in their own way, but they couldn't be deterred from their subconscious state of mind.

Ella swept past two cops who'd taken up positions of cover behind the SUV. The figure in the front seat had ducked, long, dark hair falling about his face where he cowered.

Brenner let out a long breath, turning to look up the slopes, scowling as he did.

"Did you hit him?"

He turned. Baker was approaching him now, his finger on his radio, muting it for the moment.

"Think so," Brenner said.

Baker glanced down at Brenner's holster, up again. "Quick shot. Did you see him?"

"No."

"You heard him then, before he fired?"

"I heard him fire," Brenner said, scanning the trees.

A low whistle. "And you managed to react like that? Damn, Gunn. If you weren't such an asshole, I'd buy you a drink."

"Yeah... well, Baker, if you weren't such a dipshit, I might accept."

The two men frowned at each other. Baker then glanced at the slopes. "We'll find him. If he's bleeding, whoever it is... Any idea who might've taken a shot at Ella?"

"The killer?"

Baker frowned. "Maybe. Hopefully you just winged our bad guy and saved the rest of those kids."

"You don't sound like you're counting on it."

Baker shook his head once. "In my experience, the sort of predators that go after kids aren't the type to face up against armed cops. They're too cowardly for that."

Brenner met Baker's gaze, and nodded once. "Hell... You and I might agree on something there, Matthias."

"Don't get used to it, Brenner. You're a marshal—you follow fugitives. Why not take Beckett and Marcy and head after the bastard? Bring him back if you find him."

"Sure."

"Bring him back alive."

Brenner was marching up the slope now, double-time. He called back. "If that's how I find him, I'll do my best."

"Brenner!" Baker snapped. "I'm warning you—no funny business. Just find the guy, bring him back."

Brenner didn't reply this time.

He hastened up the slope, wincing whenever he put too much weight on his right leg. But even a bum leg wasn't going to keep him back. He'd hit the bastard. He was sure of it. He'd heard the grunt, watched him swivel like a top.

He'd hit the man. Now he just had to find the trail.

He shot a look back over his shoulder towards where Ella was leaning against the front of the SUV, knocking on the window.

A strange woman, that.

Acting like she was fine. Like she hadn't nearly died.

Like there weren't others who were scared *for* her.

"Insufferable," he muttered under his breath, scowling. Ella wasn't so different from her sister as he liked to think... well, that wasn't entirely true. They were both stubborn. Both willful. But in other ways they were oil and water.

Priscilla, for one, took care of her own enemies.

Ell, he wouldn't have been surprised, tried to *befriend* hers. He shook his head, checking his weapon and walking swiftly forward as the terrain leveled out, moving between tree trunks, under snowbound foliage, breathing in the cold weather. The three cops up ahead were waiting for him, frowning back.

If Ella wouldn't head back to avoid the danger, then Brenner would simply have to find the threat himself. And do what any good overwatch did.

What, for five years, he'd done overseas.

In his time as a sniper, he hadn't lost a *single* team member while acting as overwatch. Guardian Angel, some had called him. Greased Lightning—death from the sky, others had said. If there was one thing that made Brenner proud, it was keeping all his brothers in arms safe.

Well... there was *another* thing that made him even prouder than that.

But he didn't like thinking about her. A flash of a smiling face. Laughter. *Daddy!*

He grimaced, shaking his head to dislodge the painful memory. This was why he hated cases that involved kids. It made his blood boil. He knew Baker wanted him to bring the shooter back alive, but Brenner was in a killing mood.

He marched right past the three cops, half-limping off his right leg as he did.

"Keep up," he growled, and he glared through the trees, his eyes searching for the target.

CHAPTER 8

ELLA'S GLOVES WERE TATTERED, somewhat torn. Inwardly, she was a bundle of nerves. Fear, pain, all of it.

But she didn't allow it purchase. Didn't allow herself to dwell on it. How could she?

Maddie Porter was still missing. The other survivors were still missing. Two teenagers dead so far. Susan Thompson and Jasmine Swallow.

She wouldn't allow it to be three.

Having knocked on the window to alert the boy in the SUV, she reached down and opened the door. Two cops standing near the hood of the car watched her.

She didn't look at them. Technically, Chief Baker had given her permission to interrogate Terry. Not that she needed his permission, but it was always easier to catch flies with honey.

She stared into the front seat as the door swung open and a burst of warm air swaddled her, emanating from the vents. The warm air also smelled vaguely of weed.

She glanced towards Terry Havek's left hand, which was hidden behind his large thigh, hastily smooshing something into the coin tray between the seats. He stared at her, blinked a couple of times, then did a double take.

"Holy smoke show," he said, brushing his fingers through his hair to stare at her. His eyes bugged. "Damn lady, you got a boyfriend?"

Ella blinked. Then said, "Mr. Havek?"

He chuckled. "Mister? Huh. Nah. My friends call me Terry." He twisted a bit in the seat, watching her from beneath long, greasy black bangs.

He looked confident and happy. Normally, she would've been pleased. But did teenagers running for their lives for two days in the mountains end up confident and happy? Why wasn't he scared?

Then again, she supposed the same could be asked of her. And, in Brenner's case, *had* been asked.

"Mr. Havek," she said slowly, looking him up and down. He was wearing his school uniform beneath an unzipped jacket. No sign of a tear. Then again, she could barely see the thing. "Would you mind giving me your sweater, please?" she said, then looked up, meeting his gaze.

"Wait, what?"

"Your school sweater? Please."

"I... umm... I mean, it's pretty cold."

"I'm aware. I'll only be a moment."

Now, though, some of the carefree tone had vanished. And he was shifting uncomfortably in the front seat. Was this just her imagination, or was he now slumping lower.

Terry Havek was nearly twenty, and built like an avocado. A lot of his bulk gathered around his waist, but then arose towards thin shoulders. He had a distinctly unattractive face but with a sparkle in his eyes above pockmarked cheeks that hinted at intelligence.

His long, dark hair hung low, in an imitation of a popstar do, except nothing else about the young man's appearance put up with this attempt.

"Your sweater, please," she said a bit more sternly.

"I mean... lady, it's like *really cold.*" He was now zipping up his jacket and shooting nervous looks towards where the two police officers by the hood were lingering. The heat continued to emanate from inside the vehicle.

"I have to insist, sir," she said, her voice firm, unyielding. She stepped back to gesture at the two cops.

Terry then said, "Fine! Fine, sure. Whatever. I'll show you mine if you show me yours." He wiggled his eyebrows, barely visible under his fringe.

She just watched him coolly.

"Do you mind?" he said, waving at her. "A bit of privacy wouldn't hurt."

She shrugged and half turned, glancing towards the cops. Terry shut the door and began unzipping his jacket. When he caught her looking through the window, he frowned, waving his hand as if to make her turn.

She did not. She couldn't think of any way he might *repair* his sweater in there. But perhaps he might imitate the tear and blame it on something else. So she kept her eyes on him.

And that's when she spotted the look of panic.

He was staring at her, breathing heavily, nostrils flaring. The window rolled down. "I didn't mean to!" he yelled.

She tensed.

The two cops were now pushing away from the hood, both frowning and stepping forward.

"I swear I didn't mean to!"

"Terry..." she said slowly. "Please push out of the vehicle." But he'd locked the car from the front seat where he'd been left to warm his hands on the heating vents.

Her weapon was now in her hand, but pointed low. She didn't want to point a gun at the young man. And though she had been thinking of all the teenagers as kids... Terry was almost twenty. In a way, she thought it was sort of stupid. At the turn of a clock, one day a child, the next day an adult. Voila! It happened overnight, just like magic.

One day a juvenile, slapped on the wrist. The next a murderer tried in adult court.

And out here, on the mountain, two teenagers were dead. And the young man sitting in the car, staring at her with panic in his eyes... She had to be honest.

Had he been seventeen, even just an inch on the right side of the arbitrary number, she might have had a flicker more compassion in her gaze. But nineteen? Pushing twenty.

The wrong side of the line.

This was not someone destined for a juvenile court. Perhaps it was unfair. But so was murder. Ella's weapon raised now, and she said, "Get out of the car now, sir! Please."

The young man's eyes widened in panic. And then he lunged. The door was locked, but he went for the keys to the ignition. They'd been left in the car to allow him the heat.

The cops yelled. Ella held her fire.

Her shoulders tensed—she backed away. She couldn't shoot.

Perhaps she wasn't looking at him like a young man after all—even there, desperately yelling, trying to put the car in gear, the big, bulky avocado-shaped young man looked like panicked kid.

She cursed, dropping her gun and firing at the tires.

She took one out. The car jerked. But now, shouting in panic, his voice still pulsing dully from inside, Terry Havek yanked the steering wheel, veering back onto the road, nearly hitting Ella. She flung herself to the side.

And then, he nearly hit one of the other cops.

She yelled, firing and hitting his back wheel.

He hadn't managed to keep the car straight, but instead began to reverse, picking up speed, spraying gravel and snow from the base of the spinning rubber.

He was yelling at the same time as the deflated tires screeched. Cops shouted. Ella retreated, gun still raised, now firing at the second front wheel. Another *bang!* as the tired popped. The car skidded a bit, swerving, and Ella shouted, "Don't do it, Havek! You're going off the road! Stop!"

But the young man was too scared. He sped up, racing down the hill, skidding one way then the other. She let out a huff of air and then broke into a jog, keeping pace. He continued to swerve, and then slammed into an oncoming jeep.

Horns blared. Glass scattered across the ground. Terry Havek stumbled out of the car, cursing, bleeding from his nose.

He took two paces and one of the cops raised his gun.

"Don't shoot!" Ella barked, half-spinning where she jogged. She glared the ten paces back towards where the cop was aiming. "Where's he gonna run?" She then turned again, moving faster.

The cop held his fire, thankfully. But Ella's mind was seared with Susan Thompson—tied to the tree. Dead. She pictured Jasmine Swallow, left on the cold ground. Also dead.

Some of her aversion to opening fire vanished.

"Stop, now! Stop, Terry!"

The large youth was still stumbling forward, tripping and gasping, and exhaling. She finally caught up to the much larger man, lowering her shoulder, bringing it slamming into his back and taking the two of them collapsing to the ground. She remained on top, yelling now—which was rarely her modus operandi. "Stay down! Don't move! Don't move!"

Terry Havek was crying, his large shoulders shaking. "I didn't mean to," he was saying. "I didn't know," he moaned.

With the sound of faint *clicks,* Ella cuffed the suspect.

CHAPTER 9

THEY HAD STILL ONLY found three of the kids. Two dead.

And Terry.

Ella settled across the plastic picnic table, taking one of the two folding chairs that had been provided by a search team member.

The tent surrounding them, a small pavilion, really, had been set up by the local police, creating a staging area and something of a shelter for when the blizzard began to hit. Only a few hours now until the storm was on them.

The long-haired youth sat across from her, his hair brushed back behind his ears now. One of the cops—who was standing by the door to the pavilion—had threatened to cut the bangs off if the young man hadn't cleared them from his eyes.

And now that she looked him in the face, she spotted the guilt. The fear.

But Ella always attempted to take things one step at a time. Process rather than presumption.

So she folded her gloved hands on the cold, plastic picnic table, her legs crossed. She'd always been small, and had known it. But sitting across from such a large, avocado-shaped lump, she was confident the disparity between them was emphasized.

She cleared her throat, but instead of addressing Havek, she glanced towards the cop in the door. "Any sign of Marshal Gunn?"

The cop gave a quick shake of his head. "They're still looking for the shooter. This little prick had an accomplice."

Ella hesitated, fidgeting. She didn't correct the cop on this count since all she really had was a theory.

But in her mind, she hadn't yet determined the gunman was even connected to this case. He'd come straight at her. Risking everything to shoot her dead.

The only connection she had with any of the teenagers was Maddie Porter. Perhaps someone was targeting their relatives, but this would have been a stretch.

Whereas she knew of at least one gold-miner in Nome who had a vendetta against her. More specifically, who'd threatened her to her face.

In fact, *two* had. Priscilla's exact words had been: *"You ever come near my family again... And I'll bury you under the ice, you dumb bitch!"*

Ella frowned, thinking back to her sister. The ice princess herself with a heart of snow would have to had possessed a lot of gall to speak with her and Brenner by the body while knowing all along someone was gunning for her sister.

Then again, perhaps she hadn't known. Her father was the one who'd hired gun thugs to attack Vince Longstreet *and* Tom Dilahunty the previous week. Both times, the gunmen had failed, though.

"Three strikes," she murmured, shaking her head and releasing a pent up sigh.

If she was honest with herself, she didn't *know* if her father and sister were involved in the hit. She didn't *know* the man had been targeting her.

Perhaps the cop was right. Maybe he had simply been shooting at one of the investigators near the SUV.

There was a thought. What if he'd been trying to help Havek escape?

She settled her gaze on Terry. One issue at a time. She then reached towards the plastic container at her side and withdrew the sweater. Terry was still wearing his jacket, fully zipped up now, and flinched as he set eyes on the periwinkle school sweater.

She set it on the table, pointing.

"What's this?" she said simply.

No tear. She'd looked twice. But even though there was no rip in the fabric, *there was* a red stain down the front. She tapped a finger against it.

"Tell me about this, Terry."

"I... juice."

"You expect me to believe you ran because you had juice staining the front of your sweater?"

"I mean... it's more on the side."

"Do you think comments like that are helping or hurting you here, Terry?"

"I mean, er, you nearly shot me."

Now that she was sitting across from the man, his hands cuffed behind him, his hair out of his eyes, she felt far more in control; not just of the situation, but her emotions.

One thing she'd prided herself on—suspects never riled her. She kept her cool. It was the best way to get them to reveal more than they'd intended, allowing them to compensate for her lack of reflected emotion.

Plus, it gave her a chance to pay attention to the details. The small things. For one, Terry was right. The blood stain was more to the side. Near the right side of his sweater. Susan Thompson's head had lolled to the *left*. Small details.

But Susan had bled on the left side of her chest, the blood soaking through her sweater, parting around her breast and pooling near her belt, staining her shirt.

"Did you kill Susan Thompson?" Ella asked directly, unblinking, her voice completely devoid of passion.

"What? Hell no! No—I didn't!"

"So when we run this blood for DNA. It's not going to be Susan's?"

He froze. "I—I didn't kill her!" The moan from earlier was returning to his voice.

"Help me to help you, Terry."

"Hell no, lady. I didn't do anything!"

"That's not what it sounded like earlier. You looked scared. You almost sounded like you were apologizing for something. Is there something you want to tell me?"

He stared at the table, biting his lip. "I... I want a lawyer."

"I understand," she said. "Would you like me to leave?"

"Yes!" he said.

She stood up, adjusting her jacket sleeves. "I can leave this here for you."

He stared at the sweater. And now that he wasn't wearing it, now that he was fixated on the patch of blood on his own clothing, his eyes widened. "No... no, please. Just—just take it."

"I mean... I can put it in the plastic tub here, but I'll have to stay a bit. Can we talk a bit more?"

"Just get it off the table!"

"Can I ask you a few more questions?" Technically, she was playing fast and loose with her suspect's right to remain silent. But there were more arbitrary lines than simply the court a suspect was prosecuted in. Sometimes, the rules provided, meant to keep police within the bounds, had to be bent.

There were teenagers on that mountain. A blizzard incoming. If they had found the killer... or perhaps just an accomplice to the killer, then she needed information. And she needed it now.

Thankfully, her conscience was somewhat assuaged as he nodded quickly. "Yeah... yeah, whatever. Just... I don't want to look at it." He sobbed.

She settled once more. The chair legs shifting in the rocky terrain, and small pebbles crunched under foot as she sat again. The cop by the door pretended like he wasn't paying attention, but he wore a look of approval.

Ella placed the sweater back in the tub, then folded her hands.

"Let me tell you what I think, would that be okay?"

"Whatever."

"You couldn't help yourself. Is that right? You were sleeping so close to them. Those pretty girls—the ones you always watched in school, but who never wanted anything to do with you. They brought you along because of..." she reached down and pulled the second item they'd found in his jacket. A bag of small tablets and blunts. "Because you had the *wares*. Is that right?"

"W-what? That's not mine."

"Terry," she said, leaning forward now and resting her hand on his. She smiled at him, her expression kind. "You don't have to lie to me."

He stared at her, met her eyes, looked down again. Ella knew she was attractive to him. He'd said as much in the car. But also, this close, she could see the way his nostrils flared, breathing faster. The way he swallowed, though he tried to pretend he hadn't. The way he looked anywhere but at her. She wanted to sigh in frustration. Growing up it had often been uncomfortable how her attempts to be gentle and kind could be misconstrued.

But this, she'd long ago decided, was an unfortunate complication. Something to be stepped around, rather than exploited. But she still believed in kindness, and so she left her hand, but straightened a bit.

"You can tell me, Terry. I understand what it is to have secrets. It just got to be too much. Maybe you went to tell Susan you liked her... Maybe she said something. Heck, maybe she even deserved it. Is that right, Terry? I wouldn't blame you. If she called you names? Made fun of you? Something like that?"

"No! No, that's not what happened! I didn't kill Susan!"

Ella lifted her hand, leaning back now. And she spotted in his eyes something like regret. In his mind, the reward was her touch. The punishment for his evasion was abandoning it. He leaned forward almost imperceptibly as if craving her affection once more. The details spoke to her, and this one was troubling.

She leaned back just as much. Her arms crossed, and she studied him. "So if you didn't kill her, who did? Was it a friend of yours? Someone you knew? I know your father has a criminal record, Terry."

He winced. "I... I haven't seen him for years."

"Mhmm. He got out of prison in Seattle a year ago, right? Has he come to visit recently?"

"No! No, he didn't."

"I hear he also had trouble with women. Isn't that why he was serving sixteen years?"

Terry moaned now, shaking his head. Some of his bangs fell loose again, his hair dangling past his face now. His shoulders were shaking and he looked cold. Ella felt a jolt of compassion. Naturally, her instincts were to take care of wounded creatures. To bind their limbs. It was one of the reason she had gotten along so well with Brenner—he'd always had a soft spot for animals.

Ella, on the other hand, had often had a soft spot for dangerous things. Not just animals, not just wolves and bears and lions. But also... stranger things. She could remember thinking fondly of spiders, of scorpions. And also of serial killers.

Perhaps fond was the wrong word. But her heart did sometimes break when she thought of a life destined behind bars.

It broke far more for those wounded by the killers, left to rot in shallow graves, hidden like fetid secrets. Ella knew compassion was a useful tool, but a horrible master. Compassion became tyrannical when it allowed spurts of tenderness for killers to allow them loose on their prey.

But she couldn't help herself—something about Terry Havek seemed ... *sincere*. She knew how wild it sounded. But the blood on his sweater didn't cinch it for her. He was clearly ashamed. Full of guilt. He'd clearly done something awful.

But was it murder? Was he involved? Or was something else going on here.

She tapped her fingers against her arms. Then said softly, "I know what it is to carry a secret, Terry..." A silence fell between them. Voices outside the tent suggested some of the search parties were returning now. The darkness was coming. The blizzard drawing nearer, and the shooter was still at large. Ella ignored it all. She listened to the faint whistle of the wind ushering in under the pavilion's flimsy, fabric door.

As the wind hummed, she continued, in a voice more like a murmur than anything. "It gnaws at your soul. It doesn't let you sit still. When you lay your head to rest? It's there, on your shoulder, in your ear. And it doesn't get better, Terry. It rots. It writhes with the maggots born in the poisoned memories. It then spreads, like a toxin. That guilt—those secrets, unless released, they come back. Like old enemies, looking for us when we're at our weakest." Ella glanced down at the table now, staring at the back of her gloves. She absentmindedly traced the outline of her phone through her pants pocket. "It's an odd thing," she murmured. "Very odd. Sometimes... the secret doesn't ever leave you alone. It doesn't matter how far you run, how desolate a place you retreat to... sometimes it will follow you to the ends of the Earth."

She then looked up, perky and energetic. "But I'm sure you don't know what I'm talking about. At least, not yet."

He stared at her, unblinking, as if frozen in place. He swallowed again, but this time it had nothing to do with her touching his hand.

He let out a little gasping breath. "I... I'm embarrassed," he whispered.

She leaned forward again, this time with both hands, giving his wrist a gentle little, affectionate squeeze. "I'm here for you, Terry. Would you like something to eat? Something to drink?"

"I... hamburger?"

"Why don't I see what I can do. Would you like a cheeseburger? Extra bacon?"

"Yes! Yeah..." he nodded quickly.

She patted him on the arm, like a dog trainer. She didn't say *good boy,* but she might as well have.

"I'll go get that for you, but first, talk to me, Terry." She gave a little laugh, and it scared her to realize she meant it. The emotion felt as real as if she'd been sitting across from an old friend, waxing poetic about childhood stories.

Terry even seemed to relax a bit, breathing easier. His hand had gone limp under her fingers' caress. He then closed his eyes and murmured. "I found her like that."

Ella didn't move. She stared at him, though, watching his face—his eyes closed. "Found who?"

"Susan. She was dead. I found her."

"I see... And did you see who killed her?"

"No... But James wasn't in the tent. He said I smelled."

"That's not very nice."

"No..." Terry said, his eyes still closed, nearly slumbering.

"And so where did James go?"

"I—I dunno."

"Alright. Forget about that. What did you see? Why is there blood on your sweater, Terry?"

"I kissed her."

"Excuse me?"

His eyes squeezed shut now. The look of embarrassment intensified. He was crying, shaking his head. "I... I shouldn't have. I know it. I know I'm a pervert. Just like my dad. I'm sorry. I know."

"Calm down, Terry. Calm down, it's okay." Ella had moved around the side of the table, standing next to Terry. She even bent to be at his height. Her arm wrapped around his shoulders. He did smell of skunk weed. But she didn't care. She gave him a side hug.

The cop in the door was now watching her with a look of confusion, but she ignored him the same as the stink.

"Terry, tell me what you did."

"I... I saw her tied to the tree."

"What time was this?" Ella said quickly.

"I... five-thirty."

"You're sure?"

"Yeah. I had a digital watch. I checked. Cuz James was gone so long."

"So you found Susan at five-thirty."

"I thought she was still alive! She was still moving."

"Still moving? But she was already stabbed?"

"Yes! I swear it. She was already dead… or… or at least she died when I watched. Her head sort of fell. That's why I thought she was alive. Her head moved. But then never after. I think… Oh, shit… I think I saw her breathe her last breath. Holy shit. Holy…"

"Terry, focus. So what did you do?"

"I swear I didn't know she was hurt. I thought she was playing a game with James! The two of them had been whispering at the campfire. I saw them! I saw them!" His eyes opened now, and he was rocking back and forth, shaking his head, more hair falling loose.

"That made you jealous, didn't it?" Ella whispered.

"Yes! Why… why don't they ever like me?" he moaned. "I… No one ever likes me. They all like *James!*" he yelled, angry now. "It's not fair!"

"No, no, it's not. I'm sorry. And so you saw Susan tied to the tree."

"She wasn't wearing her jacket. I thought they were playing a game… you know. Like an adult game."

"And so you went up to her?"

"It was so dark. I didn't know."

"Tell me what happened, in your own words."

Terry Havek was still crying, but he whispered, "I started teasing her. Threatened to tickle her."

"And that aroused you, didn't it? She was helpless. She had never looked at you like she looked at James… is that when you killed her?"

"I didn't! I swear I didn't. I… I swear on my mom! I didn't kill her." He was shifting now, staring at her with tear-stained eyes. His breath still smelled horribly. But she didn't recoil. Her arm still patted at his large back. She smiled at him, giving an encouraging little nod.

The effects of power, beauty, wealth and prestige had long since lost their allure. So many spent their lives chasing a mountaintop, but there wasn't enough air to share up there. Far smarter to stay in the valley—there was room enough for everyone at the base of the mountain.

"I… I teased her. Then said I would kiss her. She didn't say anything. I said if she didn't tell me not to, I was going to kiss her."

"And she didn't say anything," Ella said now, the picture settling in her mind. Her voice went grim.

"No… She was so cold. I shouldn't have… I…" He stared at her, his eyes streaked with tears. "I kissed a dead girl," he said, his voice hoarse. "I… I know she hated me. She just wanted me around for—like you said. But I liked her. I liked her a lot. I thought… thought maybe if I tried hard enough, she'd like me too."

Ella closed her eyes, letting out a little sigh. "Alright, Terry." She leaned back, giving him a final encouraging squeeze on his shoulder. "So help me, please. What happened after?"

"After?"

"Yes. The campsite. We all saw it. Susan was dead, but the campsite was ravaged. What happened?"

"Oh... I kissed her and then realized she was wet. I found blood on me, and I yelled. Then..." His eyes widened. "Then the monster showed up."

"What?"

"The Mockingbird," he said insistently.

"So... a man showed up?"

An adamant and fierce shaking of those long bangs. "No!" he insisted. "It wasn't a man. It was the Mockingbird. He's only *sometimes* a man. Before he feeds. But then he fed on Sophie and he turned into his true form."

Ella scowled. She almost reprimanded him for lying. But nothing had changed about his tone. His eyes were still wide, pupils still dilated, his fingers still trembling. He had a ghostly quality to his voice as he narrated as if speaking of something he saw far off in the distance.

Ella felt a cold shiver probe down her own back.

She said, carefully, "What did this monster look like? Could it have been a man in a large jacket? In disguise?"

He scoffed. "Is a man ten feet tall?"

"So this monster was ten feet tall?"

"It had demon eyes. Big, gold demon eyes. It was half man, half beast. It had teeth the size of my thumbs!" He jammed his hands up now, both his fingers jutting in front of his gaze, his handcuffs rattling where his fingers trembled.

Ella shook her head. "Terry... are you..."

"I'm not lying to you! I swear it! There's a monster out there. I know what I did was wrong. I shouldn't have kissed Sophie. I... I wanted to do more," he said, clearly in a confessing mood.

Ella winced. She'd heard enough. She didn't believe Terry was the killer. She said, "Look me in the eye, Terry. Do you know who did this?"

He looked her dead in the eye and said, "The Mockingbird."

"And do you know who that is?"

He shook his head adamantly. "Not a clue. And, lady, you're nice. You should leave. The Mockingbird only gets more powerful as he kills. He's going to kill everyone. Us too." He swallowed, his head dipping. "I guess I deserve that."

Ella watched him. In part, she knew he was looking for sympathy. But that didn't mean she would be stingy with it. In part, she also saw his self-loathing. Saw how much he hated what he'd done. It wasn't her job to make those choices.

But it took so very little human compassion for her to murmur. "You don't deserve to die, Terry. But you do need to do the right thing."

He looked at her, like a confessor seeking absolution. "What?" he said.

"Tell everything you just told me to that officer. Leave nothing out. Every single detail. Especially the part about the Mockingbird, okay? It could help us save the lives of your friends."

"They were never my friends," he said, bitter. "They just wanted weed."

Ella knew it wasn't right. But she thought of Brenner Gunn. *That trailer kid,* as her mother had often called him. Some people were dealt all the best cards. And others were left with a bad hand. Still, if so many people weren't so intent on climbing the mountain, it wouldn't be as bad.

It wasn't just the St. Andrews Academy kids of the world.

It was everyone who wanted to be like them, to associate with them. The dirty little secret of the Porter family's success was that *everyone,* no matter how much they grumbled and complained behind closed doors, treated the Porters like royalty.

Ella said, "If they weren't your friends, why did you come?" And then she turned, shaking her head and brushing past the cop. "Take his statement, please," she said over her shoulder, marching forward, up the slope again.

She didn't believe in mythical monsters.

But someone sure as hell did.

A ten foot monster with teeth the size of thumbs?

She knew of people in the mountains who kept the strangest pets.

"Baker!" she called out, waving a hand towards the tall cop. "Hey—I need access to your database. I need to look something up."

CHAPTER 10

THE FRONTIERSMAN GROANED, PULLING to a halt outside the Cheap and Easy motel, wincing as he did and dabbing at his bloody shoulder.

"Damn marshal," he snapped for the fiftieth time in the drive back from the mountains. He'd managed to give his trackers the slip, sneaking back towards the vehicles, using a stolen cop jacket, and then hightailing out during the vehicle shuffle.

He'd tried to follow them up by snowmobile, but the pass had been too narrow. They would have seen him coming. He cursed as he put the car in park and kicked open the door.

Then, he'd waited in ambush, willing to take the risk. The only reason he'd been able to slip away was because he'd taken the time they were up the slopes to rehearse his escape path, plant the cop jacket and prepare his getaway vehicle *three* times. And even then...

"You missed," he said, talking to himself in a murmur. "How the hell did you miss?

Then, answering his own question, also out loud, he said, "She jumped. The crazy bitch jumped off the mountain. She's probably dead."

He nodded to himself, pushing out of the car, and standing next to it, radio in hand. He'd managed to use the first-aid in the getaway vehicle to patch his arm. But it was a temporary fix. He'd have to go see Dr. Messer. The coroner didn't ask questions—she'd always had a soft spot for her hunting buddies.

But no... not yet. Messer seemed to like Ella Porter. Probably best he go find another stitch.

He glanced at the motel, wincing and scanning the doors on the second level. Some silver numbers remained, but mostly the outlines were left. Only silver—not gold. People dumb enough to steal door numbers in Nome were too stupid to realize the difference between gold paint and the real thing.

The pawn shop down the street had an interesting stack of *silver* numbers, all the same, that perfectly matched the outlines on the motel doors missing their enumeration.

He chuckled, wincing, and shook his head, pulling out his burner phone. He checked the second number that the boss had given.

"Probably just call and confirm, yeah? Before telling the boss?"

He considered this, then nodded. Instead of placing a call to Porter and letting him know the job was done—I mean, she'd jumped off the *damn* mountain—he figured it wouldn't hurt to confirm that Ella Porter had met her fateful end at the bottom of a ravine.

His call connected after two rings.

"Hey? Chief Baker speaking."

The frontiersman cleared his throat. "Hello, chief. This is County Clerk Rogers. I got your number from the DA. We just wanted to confirm rumors that the field agent with the bureau was killed on the mountain this morning.

"What the hell? There's no county clerk named Rogers. Who is this?"

"Uh, new hire, sir. Should I put the DA on?" the frontiersman winced, wishing he'd done his homework. He hadn't thought Chief Baker would know the names of county clerks.

But Baker sounded exhausted. He said, "Lose my number. Emergencies only. And no—Agent Ella Porter is fine. She's interrogating a suspect. Now, don't call." He hung up.

The man stood there, frozen in place. He scowled, looking out across the town, watching a horizon turn dark, clouds rushing rapidly in. "Alive? How?"

He'd seen her jump.

"Because you missed, dumbass. Shut up!"

He growled, twisting at his beard until it hurt. He spotted a cleaning lady staring at him, hands on a trolley full of cleaning supplies. He looked away from her determinedly, scowling at the ground. He checked the text message he'd sent to himself. Which room number was it again?

He didn't miss. He refused to miss.

Brenner Gunn had been a good shot, but he'd given Brenner the slip, hadn't he? Yeah... Yeah, he'd take care of Ella tonight.

When she came home—*if* she came home—he'd be waiting for her. And if not... the blizzard would take care of her. Either way, he'd make sure Porter paid him.

Besides, sitting in a motel room, watching dirty flicks while waiting for his target seemed a far cry better than crawling up that godforsaken mountain.

"Excuse me!" he called out, approaching the cleaning lady. "I seemed to have misplaced my key card. The name's Porter. I'm Eleanor's husband. Yeah—this one right here. This is our room. Silly me!" He gave a little laugh and leaned against the door.

The cleaning lady hesitated. But then he flashed a crisp fifty. "Maybe this will help. Don't tell my wife," he said, chuckling. "I've just... you know." He pressed a thumb to his lips and mimed as if he'd been drinking.

Spotting the fifty, the cleaning lady brightened, pulled a card from her pocket and swiped the door.

The lock clicked. The card reader turned green. And he pulled the handle, stepping into the motel room of Ella Porter.

He'd wait all night if he had to.

As the door closed behind him, he pulled his gun—checked the clip, chambered one—then locked the door and marched over to the bed.

He snatched a towel, wincing as he did, and tossed it by the door to prevent the ambient light from shining under the frame. He'd once gone on a mission where an idiot had given his position away by the glow under the door.

Once the towel wedged in place, though, he turned...

Where was that damn remote?

CHAPTER 11

Ella sat in the back of the SUV, her face illuminated by the blue screen of the laptop. The sky was darkened now, and her fingers flew across the keyboard.

"Come on... come on," she murmured to herself, and then stopped. Talking to one's self, some said, was the first sign of insanity.

She frowned, leaning in, her eyes bleary. Ahead, near the pavilion, she watched as the late night search party gathered. Some of the others had already gone home. But relatives, parents and the like were determined to head out again.

And Chief Baker had finally made the call to try again. Only two hours until the blizzard hit. And they still had four kids out there, including Maddie.

But there was all this business about the Mockingbird. Some stupid, mythical monster. She didn't believe it for one second. But she *did* believe Terry Havek had described, to the best of his ability, what he'd seen. He'd been too honest about everything else to lie about this.

Unless, of course, she was completely duped. Which wasn't out of the question.

Which was why she was now searching for anyone in Nome with a criminal record who *also* happened to have special permitting or licensing at their jobs to access dangerous, wild animals. She was also expanding the search to include cruelty to animals or crimes involving wildlife.

Already the results were flooding in. She'd been forced to head halfway down the mountain again to connect on a hotspot in the SUV for internet access.

Nome only had a few thousand residents. But, similar to much of Alaska, it was often difficult to track criminal records for ex-forty-eighters. Many from the lower states moved to Alaska to avoid their past.

She scanned the populated list of names, watching the buffering symbol continued to spin, spin, spin.

Fifty... Eighty...

Nearly a hundred names. She stared at the screen, scowling. As she scanned through the results, she realized a good number were reports from Game and Wildlife. Many also included things like stealing crabbing gear off moored vessels.

Some of the parameters she'd used had yielded weak results.

She narrowed now.

Removing anything to do with the crabbing boats. Removing any hunting license infractions. Now the list was smaller.

Twenty names.

She again double-checked based on addresses available via the DMV. A few more names were taken from the list for people who'd moved away from Nome at least a year ago. Ella scanned the few names remaining. Some, she removed based on their age. Far too old. An eighty-year-old who'd once adopted a wolf pup wasn't likely to be hunting teens in the mountains—even if the wolf pup *had* bitten his neighbor.

All said, she found herself staring at a list of ten names.

She scanned the names, one at a time. She hesitated a moment, considering her options but then narrowed once more. Removing all female offenders. It was a risk, but the psychological profile of this particular killer, like most serial killers, matched masculine traits.

Now only seven.

She kept the three female suspects to the side, intent on returning to them in case nothing resulted from the other seven. But there was a killer in the mountains. And the biggest fear she had was that the killer was hiding among them.

It was a ploy as old as time.

Killers doubling back and joining search parties and rescue teams, hiding in plain sight.

And so she cross-referenced the seven names against the list of volunteers Chief Baker had provided. One at a time, the names were pared down. Most of the suspects had work. One of them, her system said, was in jail for drunk and disorderly.

But then a small notification bubble popped up.

She stared at the name. A single name from the list. A man who had a criminal record for assault but whose job gave him access to wildlife. Bears and wolves were both on the list.

Zeke Chernow. The same man she'd seen her sister talking with earlier in the day.

The man whose daughter, Carrie, was on the mountain. Zeke had gone out with one of the earlier search parties, though. She frowned, clicking through his profile.

And then she went still.

Zeke was separated from his wife, and while it was true Carrie was his daughter, the young woman had filed a restraining order against her own father. Accusing him of violent behavior. Ella quickly read the report. Mental health issues... Heavy medications. Violent tendencies...

And he worked as a type of tagger—a man employed by researchers to track wildlife in the region, put them to sleep, then tag their ears to keep track of them.

His own daughter hated him. He had a criminal record and violent tendencies.

Ella shivered. Terry had seen a monster... But looking at a couple of the pictures of the grizzlies on the website for Zeke's employer, *Fauna Solutions,* any of these creatures would easily be close to ten feet tall if rearing on their hind legs.

Ella double-checked the information then pushed out of the SUV, hastening back up the slopes towards where the search parties were dispersing for a final search before the blizzard.

***

Brenner had lost the trail of the gunman nearly an hour ago... and he wasn't sure *how* it had happened, but now he was sucked into one of the search parties. Helping to move up the slopes in a grid pattern, doing his best to keep an eye out for any of the other kids. The request for a drone to find the gunman? Denied—needed for the search. The request for a snowmobile? Also denied.

But the gunman was gone, and Brenner had double checked with Baker that Ella was safe. Besides, he reasoned, the best way to find the gunman was to join a much larger search team...

Except this team was searching for others.

Three found so far. Susan and Jasmine both dead. Terry alive.

That left four others. Carrie, Maddie, James and Aspen. And, if he was fortunate, the missing gunman.

Brenner paused, wincing and leaning against his injured leg, kneading and massaging the muscles under the skin. The search party had lost a few members by now—citizens of Nome heading home to batten down the hatches before the storm hit. The gunman would no doubt be hunkering down as well.

But a few figures still moved ahead of him, traipsing over the mountain paths, through the snow. He let out a long breath in the form of fog and glanced back down over his shoulder. Ella was safe, according to Baker.

And as much as Brenner wanted to keep an eye on her, he also wanted to find those kids.

He looked back up the slope and began trudging forward with renewed energy. "Maddie!" a voice called out ahead of him. "Aspen!" another voice yelled.

He spotted the two figures off to his right moving down another trail.

"There's a cabin up this way," one of them said. "I've seen it in Spring."

The other nodded and the two glanced back at Brenner as if seeing whether he'd join them. Technically, the cabin wasn't in their grid, but they all knew they were on a clock. The storm on the horizon was hurtling towards them over the Bering Sea. The blizzard would be on them within the next hour or so.

Brenner just waved them on. "I'm going to check the trapper's bluff," he said. "You guys go on."

"You sure?" one of the searchers said. "Don't go far."

Brenner gave a thumbs up, and watched as the two remaining members of the search party veered off, heading up the path. Two other members, in bright orange shirts had come to a halt about ten yards back, both pausing to catch their breaths and take sips of water from the thermoses at their hips.

Brenner double-checked these searchers weren't too flagged. But the figures were pausing every other sip to chat or share some trail mix. So he decided this likely meant they were fine on their own.

Up ahead, Brenner spotted a small, flapping, orange flag—the same flags the other search teams had been given to indicate an area had already been covered. Two sets of footprints moved up towards this orange flag...

But none returned.

He frowned at the ground, studying the boot prints in the snow. Adults. One woman, one man.

"Hello?" he called up the slope.

An answering voice, "Hello! Is someone down there?"

He scowled now, biting his lip. He recognized the voice. "Priscilla?" he said, hesitant. Normally, he would've turned around and marched away. But there was a note of fear to her voice.

"God dammit!" Priscilla Porter snapped. "Do I have to write a letter or can I get a bit of help up here?"

Brenner paused, staring up the incline. The fluttering, orange flag trembled in the snow. And past it, he spotted what looked like a sled attached to the back of a snowmobile. Stuck. He wasn't able to see beyond the back half of the snowmobile, as the terrain leveled out, dipping back again, creating a minor hill, blocking his view.

Summoning his resolve, he trudged up the hill, marching towards the voice. His right leg was throbbing worse than usual in the cold, and he pressed his teeth tightly together, but there was nothing Brenner was more familiar with than pain. He'd grown up with bruises for blush, a morning administration of the punishment from his father's errant fist.

How many times had Brenner stood between his drunken old man and his mother?

Now, his mother was dead.

His father, the mean old git, still clung to life, perhaps terrified of what waited for him on the other side of death.

Brenner's teeth tightened against each other as he forced himself to march up the incline. He reached the sledge, realizing now that it was attached to a *toppled* snowmobile.

His heart quickened and he took a couple of hurried steps forward.

"Cilla?" he said. The word felt like lemons on his tongue. He'd avoided that name whenever he could.

Priscilla Porter was huffing, blowing air and trying to push out from under the snowmobile. Her left leg was trapped, but she'd made good progress in extricating it, judging by the widening shelf of snow packed down around her.

Priscilla glanced up at him and then froze. "You."

"Yeah, me. What the hell are you doing—why weren't you calling for help?"

Priscilla pointed at him. "I just did, pretty boy. Now lift the damn sled."

Brenner crossed his arms and shrugged. "Say please."

She glared at him.

A strange thing to see such unbridled anger in those eyes. Ella Porter and her twin sister Priscilla couldn't have been more disparate.

Ella guarded her emotions like gold in the US mint. She rarely allowed a true glimpse of her inner thoughts to be seen. She used politeness, smiles, gentleness, like weapons, tools. She *was* kind but also used it. She *was* gentle but also employed it. Ella bought things secondhand. Even her new jacket had worn sleeves.

Priscilla, on the other hand, was cold-hearted and dead inside. Then again, perhaps he was somewhat biased on this subject.

Others, perhaps a bit more charitable than Brenner, might have suggested Cilla Porter wore her heart on her sleeve. When angry, people knew it. When happy, people also knew it. She was loyal to her father. Loyal, also, to Chief Baker.

But Brenner knew her better than that. Cilla was loyal to power most of all.

Instead of saying *please,* Cilla just kept kicking, wiggling and desperately trying to dislodge her own leg, grimacing in pain as she did.

"Stubborn as hell, you know that?" Brenner said. He shook his head, bent over and began tugging at the sled. He winced a couple of times but then managed to tip it forward, which relieved some of the pressure from the machine braced against Priscilla's leg.

No sooner had she been unpinned than the woman scrambled to her feet.

"Were you alone up here?" Brenner asked.

"No, don't be dumb." She brushed hurriedly at her coat, sending flurries to the ground. Clearly, she was embarrassed, which necessarily meant she was pissed at anyone watching her.

Brenner didn't look away. "Who else is up there?"

"He said he was going to plant the flag. Took him like thirty minutes, so I went to get him, and this stupid, idiotic machine tried to kill me."

"Someone's still up there?"

Priscilla snorted, looking at him now, hands on her hips. "Did you hear a word I said?"

"What? Wasn't listening."

Brenner began to move past her, marching up the slope, looking for any sign of the missing search team member. As he passed by her, without so much as a glance, Priscilla caught his arm.

He ripped his wrist away and growled like a wounded bear. "I told you not to touch me!" he snapped, glaring at her.

He was standing too close and let out a fluttering little breath. She really was just as pretty as her sister. But the eyes made the difference. Those were cold eyes. Eyes that didn't carry the same warmth as Ella's.

Eyes, he guessed, that had gone cold around the same time his heart had.

They'd both suffered the same loss, after all.

"You know you can't keep following her around like a puppy dog," Priscilla said, and her voice had a strange note to it that Brenner couldn't quite place at first. Tenderness? Concern? He scoffed at the thought.

"Don't know what you're talking about." He tried to push past her, and she caught his wrist again, and this time he yanked harder, sending her stumbling a step.

Now, the tenderness in her voice vanished, and the usual tempest returned. "What the hell do you think is gonna happen, Brenner? When she finds out what you did, she'll never speak to you again!"

"What *I* did? That's rich."

Priscilla shrugged, adjusting her jacket now. She didn't have the decency to look at the ground, but instead, met his eyes with a belligerence that made his blood boil. "You did it. You wanted to just as much as me!"

"*Did* it? Hah—you make it sound like I'm the one who tricked you."

"Oh *please*!" Cilla snapped, flinging a hand up and sending a few clumps of slush splattering across the snowmobiles windshield. She shook her head, grumbling now, and adjusting the handlebars, double-checking everything was still attached. She then shifted forward, wincing on her leg but trying to straddle the machine.

Brenner didn't help her. But he could feel old memories surging back. Anger rising in his chest so fast that he wanted to scream. "You tricked me."

"That? I'm not talking about that, Brenner. And you know it. Fine—I stole a kiss. So what? I just wanted to see what it was like. I mean... you might be a trailer kid, Brenner, but you were hot. I'll give you that."

She was now sitting on the snowmobile, head high, imperious. Very much like her mother. Very much as if the machine beneath her was some sort of throne, and Brenner just some serf who didn't deserve a second glance.

"Ella saw us—saw me kiss you."

"Oh God, Brenner. Let it go. It was like, what, twenty years ago?"

"Twelve. Twelve years."

Priscilla shook her head. "You're the one who broke up with her. Fair game as far as I saw it."

He went quiet, seething, remembering that night. He'd been drinking. It had been late. His heart had been in agony since breaking up with his childhood crush. Ella Porter had always seemed too good to be true.

He'd thought he was going to ruin it. Had felt as if he'd never deserved her. And so he'd pushed her away.

It had been a particularly brutal night back at his house. He'd realized that Gunn men were simply monsters. He'd had a dream... A dream where he'd treated Ella the way his father had treated his mother. And in that dream, he'd heard Lois and Jameson Porter. Laughing... *Trailer park kid.*

He'd known Ella's parents had hated him. He'd known that he was a liability. He'd been drinking again...

And so he'd broken up with Ella. But then three weeks later... He'd realized what a huge mistake he'd made. He'd returned to the Porters' residence, braving the disapproval of the parents.

And Priscilla had answered the door.

"You told me you were going to get Ella."

"What?" Cilla said something else, gunning the engine, but then muttered darkly, "Not working."

"I said—" Brenner snapped, grabbing her by the arm now and pulling sharply.

She turned to look at him. Her smirk was back, and she glanced down. "There's the Brenner I know," she muttered. "Like daddy like son, huh?"

He wanted to squeeze, but he forced his hand to release and stepped back, guilt surging through him. "You're a witch."

"Cauldron bubble, baby," she said with a wink. "Now here, give it a push. I think it's stuck."

"You told me you were going to get Ella."

"Yeah. I said a lot of things, Brenner. God dammit," she snapped. "I was a kid too. Alright? I thought you were cute, so I snuck a kiss. Sue me."

It would have been a tragic, sweet, heart-breaking tale. He could, perhaps, have even cast himself as the good guy. The down-on-his luck tramp, fought over by two beautiful sisters.

In his mind, he liked to play out such roles. But they were pretend.

And everyone knew it. Most of all himself.

"I shouldn't have married you," he said.

Cilla chuckled, dismounting the snowmobile now and giving a shrug. "To hell with it. Let it rot." She turned and began marching down the hill again.

Brenner glared after her, his gloved hands clutched into fists. "You were the worst mistake I ever made!"

She spun as she walked, very much how Ella so often did. Still moving, shuffling back, as if too determined to press on to come to a full halt. Cilla glared up at him. She shot a look towards where the other search members were still munching on trail mix, but she made no effort to keep her voice down.

"You wanted me too, Brenner. You're the one who asked me out."

"Because I wanted Ella," he snapped back, intending the words to wound the same as hers had.

"Don't you think I know that? I was twenty. I was dumb. Four years I thought about that kiss. You've always been a good kisser, Brenner." She made a sort of jutting motion with her hips. "Though the marriage bed left something to be desired..." She tapped a finger against her lips. "Maybe that's why I left you... Hmm... Who knows? I'll let you know if I reach a conclusion, because Brenner... I don't really think about you much. Four years of marriage. It was nothing. The length of a college degree."

Priscilla turned again, raising both of her middle-fingers and walking away.

Brenner stared after her. "She wasn't nothing..." he murmured. "She *wasn't nothing*!" he yelled.

Daddy! Smiling eyes, a dimpled smile.

The one thing he'd done right in the world.

But their daughter had been taken too.

That was why she'd divorced him. She still felt the pain of it. Just as much as he did. Priscilla... had been different then. In a way, it had almost felt as if she'd wanted to explore beyond the bounds of her family's expectations. To pursue something as radical as *love*. With someone her parents didn't respect.

The two of them had been so lonely after Ella had left. After a few years, they'd found solace in each other. Married far too quick. A child just as quickly.

And then the child's death.

The divorce.

And the deadness in his chest. Joining the navy, joining the Marshals.

It didn't fix it.

And never would.

He glared after her retreating form, flashing a middle-finger of his own, and then kicked the snowmobile. But instead of retreating after her, he moved up the trail, past the fluttering orange flag.

The adult male's footprints led this way.

"Hey!" Brenner called out, irritated. "Hey—the blizzard is coming. Baker wants everyone back at base camp!"

He moved quickly now, following the footprints over another hill. And then he came to a stop, frowning. A dusty old wooden cabin settled against a backdrop of scrubby trees. One of the cabin windows was shattered. The door was gouged with the marks of a claw.

"Hello?" he said, louder as he tentatively approached the cabin. "Hey—are you in there?"

He wished he'd paused to ask Priscilla the name of the moron stumbling off on his own in the mountains.

But then, a creaking sound. The door opened. A figure emerged.

"Hey, Brenner, right?"

Brenner stared at the man. The fellow in question was wearing a large, puffing jacket made of fur, or at least a very impressive imitation. He had on thick boots and a large bowie knife jutted from a sheath at his hip. He also wore a camo cap instead of a hood, and his gloves were made of a thinner, lightweight material.

The man displayed an impressive beard and reddish brown hair. Balding, apparent even under the brim of that cap, the man's face was sun-stained, suggesting he spent a good amount of time outdoors.

He was also hastily hiding something in his jacket pocket, slipping it out of sight.

Brenner hesitated. "Zeke, right?" he said slowly. "Mr. Chernow?"

Zeke Chernow nodded once, wiping a hand across his mouth. He jutted a thumb towards the cabin. "Nothing in there," he said, a bit too quickly.

"Mhmm," Brenner said, glancing up. By the looks of things, the roof had caved in... The wood, though, visible over the ceiling beams, was white—fresh breaks then.

"Did you fall through the roof?" Brenner said.

"Wha—nah, man. Not me. Nothing in there, like I said."

"Yeah. You did say that."

Brenner was still breathing a bit too heavily, his pulse still quick after his conversation—if it could be called that—with his ex-wife.

"Say, man. We should get going, yeah?" Zeke gestured towards the trail as if attempting to shoo Brenner down it.

"Yeah... Hey, what's in your pocket?" Brenner said suddenly.

"Ummm... huh?"

"You just slipped something in your pocket, and you look guilty as hell, Zeke. I don't mean to be an ass, and frankly, some of the people I've been around recently say I need to be less blunt. But god damn, Zeke, you're tweaking me out. What's in the pocket?"

Zeke stared at him now, blinking, his eyes red-ringed. "Dude... my daughter's up here. I don't have time for this shit." He began to march forward now, but Brenner noted the way his hand migrated to the hilt of his knife.

"Hang on," Brenner said quickly, holding out a hand. "Why don't you stay there a second."

"Hell, no, man!"

Brenner quickly withdrew his badge. "US marshal, sit your ass down! *Now!*"

But the magic words didn't work. Mr. Chernow continued forward, fiddling with the handle of his large, twelve-inch knife. The blade was nearly long enough to impale a man straight through.

"Hey! Hey, stop!" Brenner snapped. His gun was now in his hand, pointing. Things were escalating too quickly. "Just show me what's in your pocket, asshole!"

Zeke went still, cursing and staring at the gun. He shook his head, his eyes narrowed. "You're a prick, you know that?"

"Did you leave something in that cabin back there?" Brenner said firmly. "What's back there, Zeke?"

He knew he was right. He knew this man was hiding something. Acting strange—cagey.

Zeke just shrugged. "Man, I can show you—nothing."

Brenner hesitated. Then he nodded towards the pocket. "What's in there?"

Zeke's hand emerged, quavering now. In fact, it wasn't the only part of him that was moving wobbly. A few of his steps through the snow had also proven to be unbalanced.

And now, the source was revealed.

A small bottle, nearly empty, of whiskey.

Zeke was jutting his lip out petulantly, shaking his head. "Damn, man. It was just a couple of sips. I get the bends, dude—if I don't, you know... take a break now and then. Shit... you don't gotta be like that."

Baker had forbidden drinking during the search. This, perhaps, explained the guilt. The awkward behavior. It certainly explained the faintly slurred words.

Brenner let out a slow sigh, lowering his gun. He shook his head. "Sorry, Zeke. I'm just jumpy is all. We're all trying to find your daughter and the others."

"Yeah... yeah, that's alright!" Zeke said, looking relieved. He even attempted a smile but couldn't quite seem to figure out which facial muscles to use.

He gave a nonchalant shrug, though, and began to move back down the mountain slope.

Brenner paused, hesitant. "Say... Zeke?"

"Mhmm?" The man with the fur coat went still, a few paces away from Brenner, facing down the slope now. He didn't keep moving like the Porter sisters did.

"Why don't we... why don't we check out that cabin again."

Zeke looked back, wrinkling his nose. "I told you. Nothing there."

"Yeah... yeah, but maybe a fresh set of eyes could help." Brenner gave a nonchalant shrug, glancing again towards the roof. He spotted a few pieces of wooden splinters along Zeke's jacket. "You sure you weren't on the roof, man?" he said.

Zeke shook his head and let out a burp. He clearly didn't want to head back to the cabin. But Brenner said, "Why don't you show me. Please?"

Please... God damn, he was starting to sound like Ella.

Then again, *this* magic word seemed to work.

Zeke shrugged with a petulant little huff, and then turned on his heel and marched, with wobbly steps, back towards the small, ruined cabin. As they drew nearer, Brenner spotted *other* tracks in the snow. He frowned, bending over. "Hey... did you see these?"

"What's that?"

"Right here..." Brenner was now staring at the ground, poking his finger against impressions in the snow. "These aren't your prints... They're too small. Two sets of them."

Zeke was off behind Brenner now. "Carrie's?" he said, his voice shaking.

"Maybe... I dunno, sorry. But they head towards the cabin and then... This is *not* a teenage girl's footprint." Brenner paused, glaring now and straightening. A large footprint. He placed his own for reference, and the paw was nearly as wide as his foot was long. The claw marks gouged through the snow, into the thin layer of earth beneath.

"What is that?" Zeke said, leaning in next to Brenner.

"Bear," Brenner said slowly. He turned, glancing over his shoulder. "Mind standing where I can see you?"

"Oh... yeah, sure, man. Sure... See, look, here... Nothing in the cabin."

The man took the steps up, pushed open the door and waved inside.

Brenner frowned and followed up the steps. He spotted a few other prints in the snow, but they were disheveled, suggesting someone had dusted over them, or *ran* over them. He reached the open door to the log cabin, peering inside.

It was a mess. Broken tables, broken chairs. Floorboards shattered. In one corner, a small fire had been built but was now doused.

He also spotted dark stains in the wood, and he leaned in, staring.

"Damn... I didn't see that. Is that blood?" said Zeke from where he remained standing outside the cabin.

Brenner shook his head slowly. "No. No, this is coal. Someone must have been bored—they were drawing with coal."

"Huh…" Zeke's voice shook again. "Any sign of Carrie? Man… my eyes must be getting old. I didn't even see the coal."

But Brenner straightened, looking around. "Someone was hiding out here… No clue who. But…" he pointed ahead. "Looks like they went through that window."

"So… so no one was killed here? No one like… like maybe abducted and taken somewhere else?"

Brenner turned slowly, studying the strange man in the big, puffy coat. "There something you know you're not telling me, Zeke?"

But Zeke's fingers fluttered near his chest. "Wh-me? No! No, of course not!"

Brenner had left the SAT phone back for Ella's use. He raised his own phone, checking for a signal, but there was none up here. He shook his head and then said, "You should head back. Blizzard is coming."

"Right on, man. Are you coming too?"

Brenner shook his head, glancing towards the shattered window. "Someone went that way. I'm going to see what I can find."

CHAPTER 12

ELLA FACED CHIEF BAKER and could feel blood rushing to her cheeks. "What do you mean *no*?"

Baker said, "I mean no, Ella. That's nothing—you need *evidence* to arrest a man."

Ella waved the screen on her phone for him to see again. She'd sent a screenshot of the search parameters she'd used to locate Zeke Chernow's name. "This *is* evidence, Baker. It might not be concrete. It might only be circumstantial, but it's evidence, and it's all we have. We've got... *maybe* an hour left before the blizzard. If the killer is up here... *with* us, maybe he's sabotaging our efforts to find them."

"Find the kids?"

"Or what's left." Ella grimaced as she said it, but she knew *someone* had to say what the others were thinking. For nearly the full day now they'd been searching for the four remaining campers with no luck.

And if someone *was* sabotaging the search efforts, then the chances were it was someone on the inside with the rescue parties. She tapped a finger against her screen against the name again. Zeke Chernow.

"Where is he?" she said, keeping her tone in check and inhaling to calm herself. "I can go find him myself."

"Where's who?" a new voice said.

Ella and Baker both turned to find a bearded man with reddish hair staring at the two of them, wearing a big, puffy coat made of faux fur, by the look of it.

Zeke Chernow blinked a couple of times, scratching at his thick beard and flicking droplets of melted snow off his fingers. He'd removed the glove on his right hand, gripping it now in his left. The same hand, holding the glove, was absentmindedly tapping at a zipped pocket as if making sure something within was still there.

"Did you find Carrie?" he asked, and his voice was slurred.

Ella turned now, her hand migrating towards the cuffs in her belt. She brushed aside the frayed hem of her secondhand jacket for easier access. "Mr. Chernow, sir," she said uneasily. "I'd like to speak to you, sir."

"Ella," Baker growled, "Not now. We're evacuating."

She shot the chief a sidelong glance. She knew how difficult it was for her twin's husband to give Ella even an inch of ground. It went against every instinct he'd been trained to cultivate. "I'm just doing my job, Chief."

Baker muttered beneath his breath, then said, "Zeke—go speak with Ms. Porter here."

Mr. Chernow nodded slowly, shifting from side to side. He glanced down the trail, then said, "Where's Terry?"

"Who?" Baker said.

"Terry Havek. The survivor," he murmured. He was speaking with a faint slur and seemed to be having a hard time staying upright.

Chief Baker was growing more irate now as he waved in other members from the various search parties who seemed to have separated from their group. "I told you to stick together!" he yelled. "There—no—*there*. Put the extras in the box. The one by the tent—yes. *Thank* you." He shook his head, grumbling and moving off now.

As he strode away, carried by his lanky gait, the wind began to pick up, whistling through the mountains with higher cadence. Clearly, he didn't take Ella seriously enough to even *consider* her lead as accurate. Ella tugged at the edge of her hood, shielding her face but kept her eyes on Zeke. "Sir, I need to ask you a few questions. If you could come with me, please."

The man with the wild beard stared at her, his eyes red. "Where's... where's Terry?" he muttered.

But Ella shook her head. "Why is that important…"

Zeke was looking past her now.

Terry Havek had finished giving his statement to the police officer in the tent and they'd placed him back in the police SUV. This time in the back, in cuffs. They didn't want to risk another chance that he might try and drive the thing over one of them again.

But Zeke seemed to have spotted the figure in the back seat. He stared, swallowing. "Found their voices…" he muttered, his words slurred.

Ella stared at him. Her fingers tensed on the cuffs. Chief Baker was now directing traffic, pointing people back towards their vehicles. "Come on—now!" Baker was yelling. "Back down the mountain. Get in your cars and *go*. Now! Don, dammit, you're blocking the others. Go—hurry up!"

Figures began depositing red flags and reflective vests into the appropriate containers, and then began to move, following the barked instructions. Trees were now shifting and swaying like masts in a storm caught by the rising wind. Speckles of snow fell, stinging Ella's cheeks, her exposed nose. She exhaled slowly, feeling her breath warm her nostrils.

"Hey, Mr. Chernow. Come this way, sir."

He spotted the cuffs, tensed. He swallowed slowly. Other police throughout the area were distracted now. The rising wind, the incoming blizzard—like a mark of tar across the sky—the chaos of the search parties dispersing, many of them relatives of the missing teens, the tears pouring from their eyes caught by the caress of the frigid air.

Figures hastened past Ella and Mr. Chernow, keys jangling in gloved hands, jackets swishing as they moved hastily towards their parked vehicles.

And then, the sound of screaming. Ella turned sharply, looking up towards where Chief Baker was gesturing at three figures. Two of them in orange. One smaller, thinner. A girl with dark hair, breathing heavily. She was sobbing horribly, and the two figures on either side of her were also crying tears of joy.

Another, older woman, twenty paces away had emitted the scream. The older woman had been returning with one of the mountain search parties, but the moment her eyes landed on the young woman between the two red vests, she'd emitted the yell, tossed her red vest to the ground and broken into a sprint.

"Mom!" said the crying girl.

The older woman caught the younger in an embrace. "Aspen! Oh, thank—Aspen—holy... Are you okay? Are you?"

Ella recognized the face of Aspen O'Connor. One of the missing campers. She felt a jolt of elation. Another survivor. And another potential witness.

Zeke Chernow, though, was now moving. He was shooting looks of contempt down towards where Havek sat in the back of the car, but when Aspen arrived, his expression of loathing turned to her.

It all happened in a flash.

Some of the other searchers were continuing towards their vehicles, their gazes carrying looks of concern for the oncoming storm. Still others shot looks back at the reunited mother and daughter, smiling, or giving weary shakes of their heads in relief. Ella heard more than one muttered prayer and just as many expletives. "About damn time." "Holy shit—they found one."

But Zeke Chernow was now moving. A flash of silver, and Ella spotted a large knife appear in his hand. He began running suddenly, sprinting towards Aspen O'Connor.

Ella yelled. "Hey! Stop him!" Panic burst in her chest. She raised her gun quickly, but there was no clean shot. Too many volunteers were moving down the trail towards the parked vehicles.

"Baker!" Ella screamed. "Baker, Zeke!"

But the chief didn't hear her. Zeke didn't slow. Aspen and her mother were too distracted, too elated to notice the large man in the puffy coat charging towards them, knife raised.

Ella was already running, but she was too far behind. She raised her gun, firing into the air.

People screamed. Many ducked. Zeke kept going... No choice. Ella had to risk it. Too many people, but if she didn't, Zeke was about to stab at the O'Connors.

Ella aimed; began to squeeze.

And then. *Crack! Crack!*

Two gunshots.

Ella froze, her finger still caught on the trigger—she hadn't fired. Not her gun. But Zeke stumbled and hit the ground, knife clattering. He let out a little gasp and then went still.

Ella panted, her feet moving slower now as her head swiveled, desperately searching for—

"It's alright folks. It's alright—head to your cars. We're fine!"

Priscilla's voice echoed out from the tree line. The heiress to the Porter empire sauntered past her husband. She paused long enough to squeeze him from behind and wink. And then, gun still in hand, wearing a look like she was out for a Sunday stroll on the beach, she came to a stop by Zeke's corpse.

The O'Connors were frozen, tears still on their faces but terror in their eyes. Zeke had only been five feet away from them. The bowie knife, a twelve-inch, monster of a blade had clattered across the ground and now rested directly against Aspen's foot.

Priscilla stopped by them, bent over and picked up the knife. She paused, looking Aspen in the eyes. Then, tucking the knife in her belt, causing her jacket to bunch, she reached out, touching Aspen on the arm. "It's going to be okay now," Cilla said softly. It was a tone Ella didn't often hear from her twin. A kind, comforting tone.

Cilla patted the young teenager on the elbow. "No one's going to hurt you now. I promise." Then, as if to emphasize the point, she turned and marched towards where Zeke lay motionless on the ground.

She prodded the man with her boot, then gave a faint grunt.

Ella approached tentatively, moving between murmuring volunteers. Baker was calling over other officers while simultaneously attempting to direct the volunteers back down the hill towards their vehicles.

Ella stared at her suspect. "Is he dead?" she asked, her voice shaking.

Priscilla prodded the man again with her boot. "Looks like," she said.

Chief Baker hastened over now, putting an arm around his wife's back and pushing her aside. "Cilla, please—people are watching. It's okay, everyone!" he shouted out. "Self-defense. Go on!"

Cilla chuckled, shaking her head; she planted her feet, causing her husband to lag as well, and then went on her toes to plant a kiss on his cheek. "You're cute when you're trying to protect the department's reputation. You know that?"

"Oh, no, honey. I'm just worried about you. Are you okay?"

"I'm fine," she said. "Never better. Who was that guy—oh... Zeke? Damn."

The O'Connors, Aspen still trembling, were helped past the body with hurried footsteps by another volunteer who'd arrived with a blanket.

Ella could feel her skin prickling now. She stared at the body on the ground, dropping to a knee and extending a hand. "You killed him," she said slowly, looking at her sister.

"I saved Aspen," Cilla snapped back. "Don't get sentimental."

You shot my only suspect, you arrogant shrew! Ella thought. Out loud, she said, "I see. Well..." She pushed up slowly. "He was a suspect in all of this. Your husband," she said, keeping her tone neutral, "didn't feel as if there was enough evidence to arrest him."

Baker frowned at her. Priscilla just said, "Well... case solved then. Honey," she said, turning, "I think I'm going to go back up and look for another half hour or so."

Baker stared at his wife, horrified. "Cilla—the storm is arriving in the hour." He spread his fingers out against the sky, indicating the approaching darkness.

She nodded. "I can see that," she said. "But we've still got Maddie out there." Her eyes narrowed, and then she glanced at Ella. "You'd like our cousin. She's a bit like you, now that I think of it. Not that you would know."

Ella said. "I need Zeke's phone."

Baker was just shaking his head, looking like a man overwhelmed by a flood of input. He was pointing at a couple of officers, directing them towards the body. "Use the tent to secure it. We'll get the coroner *back* up after the storm passes. Where is Dr. Messer?"

The response was lost in the rising wind. And Ella reached down, taking Baker's lack of refusal as permission. She rummaged around in the man's pockets, trying to avoid disturbing the body too much. She found a pocket-knife, a small flask and a small bag of bait.

She wrinkled her nose, letting out a gagging sound. "What's that?" she muttered. She glanced at the side of the bag and read, out loud, "*Zeke's Miracle Bear Bait.*"

"Bear bait?" Cilla said, stepping away from her husband. She moved quicker now, caught, in Ella's opinion, between a desire to show off for her sister and a rising sense of urgency to find their missing cousin.

Ella wiggled the package. "Bear bait."

"You saw the campsite, right?"

"Slashed tent. Disheveled campsite. Yeah. And Terry Havek mentioned a ten-foot-tall monster attacking the camp."

"Bears... So Zeke did this?"

Ella stared at the dead man, sighing. "That was what I hoped to ask him about, Cilla."

"Don't take that tone. Would you have preferred I let him stab Aspen?"

Ella hesitated, shaking her head. "Why? Why attack Aspen? Why attack Susan? Any of them?"

More car doors slammed down the mountain. Headlights flashed, tires whirred as vehicles turned and made a hasty retreat along the narrow roads, hoping to outrun the storm and reach their homes before the blizzard hit. Already, they were cutting things closely.

Ella glanced at the sky, more snowflakes, small gnat-sized things, striking her nose and cheeks. She blinked a few times, trying to think clearly.

"What's the motive..." Ella said, shaking her head.

Baker was breathing a bit easier now that most of the volunteers had fled. Even the O'Connors were out of sight. The car with Terry Havek in it was being moved down the mountain.

Ella frowned. "I need to speak with Aspen."

Baker said, "Later. Now we all need to get moving."

But Priscilla and Ella both shook their heads simultaneously. They each stopped the motion almost as swiftly when they realized they were in danger of mirroring the other.

"Can't," Cilla said, determined to speak first. "Maddie is still out there. So are those other two kids."

Baker groaned. "Honey—they're either dead or in shelter. We need to do the same."

"Be dead?"

"No—find shelter!"

Ella was pacing around the body now, staring down. The first girl, Susan Thompson had been killed yesterday morning. The campsite had only been found *this* morning. Which meant Zeke had been given plenty of time to hunt the others.

Ella hesitated. "He has a parole officer, right?"

"Who?" Baker said.

"Zeke?" Cilla asked. "I didn't know he was a criminal."

"Funny," Ella said, and then instantly caught herself.

"What's funny?"

"No, nothing."

"Funny that I called him a criminal? What? Are you implying *I'm* a criminal, dear sister?"

"Never," Ella replied testily.

"Because if you ask me, your jacket is a crime against my eyes. Did you get that rancid thing off a hobo?"

"I bought it on—wait... what?"

"Your jacket. It's gross."

"No... no, the rancid..." Ella's frown wrinkled now, remembering something Terry had said.

"What?"

"I'm... just... I need to speak with Zeke's parole officer. Since I can't speak with *him*."

"Mighty passive-aggressive of you, princess. Like I said before, should I have *not* shot him?"

But Ella was now moving away, fishing the SAT phone Brenner had left her from her pocket while pulling up her smartphone, which had the criminal records downloaded of the various suspects she'd found.

She scanned down to the entry for the PO, quickly found the number, and then, pacing towards her SUV, she made the call, the phone ringing brightly in her ear. The darkness across the sky continued to spread.

And the snow continued to tumble, the flakes thickening as they carpeted the mountain in ice.

"Just leave the damn case alone for a second!" Priscilla shouted out.

Ella just shook her head, holding up a finger. "Hello?" she said. Someone had answered on the third ring.

"Apologies, but who is this?"

"My name is Agent Eleanor Porter. I'm with the FBI office in Nome—one of your parolees is named Zeke Chernow, is that right?"

A pause. "I may need a badge number, agent."

Ella rattled off the requested information. But Priscilla was now shouting at her again. "Who the hell cares about your damn murderer—our cousin is on that mountain, Ella! What are you even doing?" Cilla yanked her arm away from Baker, who kept grabbing at her elbow. She pointed at him. "Stop!" she snapped. And the Chief of Police held up his hands, his face red.

More lights flashed from down the mountain road. And now nearly all the vehicles had left.

"Sorry," Ella said quickly. "Did you get that? No—no, not that. That's my, umm... sister."

"You never did care about family," Priscilla was yelling. "God damn it, Baker—touch me again and I'll break your nose. Give me ten of your guys. We're going back up."

Ella was now struggling to focus. Her sister was berating her husband now, and Ella was trying to listen to the parole officer. Also, her stomach was twisting. Guilt in her gut. She hadn't been nearly as focused on finding those children... rescuing Maddie... as she'd been on catching the bad guy.

She froze in place, shivering. Did that mean she was in the wrong? Was Cilla—horror of horrors—*right* about something?

Ella pressed her teeth together. "Sorry, could you repeat that?"

"Of course, Agent Porter. I was just saying that Zeke was a model parolee. He always checked in on time. Our last meeting was yesterday, in fact."

"Okay... yesterday. Do you have a time for that? Location?"

"I can double check. Mind if I give you a quick call back? A few minutes tops?"

"Umm, yeah. Sure. Please make it quick."

Ella hung up, turning to where Priscilla had now marshaled the remaining cops. Most of them were shivering, faces red, hands jammed in pockets. Many of them looked bone-tired, exhausted from a day of weary labor.

But Priscilla was pointing at each of them in turn. Her gun was still clutched in her right hand, thankfully this was pointed at the ground.

But her voice was raised, even higher than the rising wind. A tempest against a blizzard, Priscilla shouted, "We're going back up. No—don't you say a damn word Garner. I'll kick your ass myself. Thirty minutes. Tops. And we find them this time. Go fast. Ignore the marked locations. And use your goddamn voices. James, Maddie and Carrie are still out there. Now go—let's go people!"

Priscilla shot a disgusted look at her sister, then strode off again, moving back up the slopes, hurling abuse at anyone lollygagging behind.

Ella scowled, taking a couple of steps after them. Maybe Cilla was right. By catching the killer or finding out who was involved in deterring the search efforts, she'd hoped that she might be doing her job.

But... she hadn't spent much time looking for the missing campers. In a way, the thought ate at her.

She began to move after her sister now, resigned to another half hour or more on the slopes. As she moved up the trail, behind the team, she even gave a weak, little call of, "Maddie?"

Other voices were calling out now. "James? Carrie?"

Priscilla led the charge, still marching and refusing to slow. They passed a row of fluttering, orange flags planted by the prior round of search parties.

It was only as she quickened that Ella realized she hadn't seen Brenner in some time. She frowned, glancing back down the slopes towards where his car was parked. Still there.

"Priscilla?" she shouted out. "Where's Brenner?"

Her sister didn't look back, but steam erupted over her shoulder as she snapped, "Who the hell knows. Maddie! Maddie, where are you?"

Ella's SAT phone began to ring, and she shivered, shaking her head. "Hello?"

"Yes, Agent Porter."

"Yeah—did you find it?"

"I just wanted to double check my notes. Zeke Chernow was with me yesterday morning at four in the morning at the Harbor Cafe. It's near where he works, and I made an exception for the early hour."

Ella paused now, and a couple of snowflakes as large as the nail on her thumb melted on her phone. "Umm... That's not possible."

"Pardon me?"

Ella shook her head. "You must be mistaken. The Harbor Cafe at five? Five AM?"

"Yes. Like I said, an exception was made."

"No... no, hang on." Ella blew a snowdrop from her lips. "How long did the meeting last?"

"It was two hours. We had some drug tests we needed to go over and retake."

"Two... The Harbor Cafe near the northern port?"

"Yes... is everything alright, Agent Porter?"

"No... No, it isn't. He couldn't have been there."

"Why not?"

Ella remembered what Havek had said. Checking his watch. The murder had been fresh at five-thirty in the morning. A half-hour after Zeke would have been meeting his parole officer.

"Because," Ella said, "The Harbor Cafe is a two *hour* drive from where I am right now. He... he couldn't have been there."

"I'm sorry... but he was."

"Are you sure it wasn't someone who looked like him?"

"Positive. I've been Zeke's parole officer for years."

Ella cursed, lowering her phone, the cold trembling up her arms. Zeke couldn't have killed Susan. But he *had* attacked Aspen, she'd seen it with her own eyes.

What the hell was going on here?

If Zeke hadn't killed Susan... and maybe not even Jasmine... then *who* had?

CHAPTER 13

Maddie Porter watched the storm come in, hiding in the barn near the small commune. She couldn't feel her feet, and she'd been running for what felt like an hour. She lay back in the sparse straw, breathing plumes at gaps in the poorly insulated, wooden ceiling.

Through the open doors of the barn, she spotted a dark blur of clouds speeding across the horizon, ushered forward by the wind. The howling gales were growing louder, and she shivered every time a new chorus of mountain moaning reached her.

But she couldn't stopper her ears. Not now.

Not when *it* was still on her trail. She'd seen things moving behind her, chasing her. Carrie was dead. She'd seen the monster land on her friend. Susan was dead, back at camp. Had the others made it?

She had spotted the barn ages ago. She knew that there were inhabited buildings a few miles down the road. Off-gridders. The sort of people who stuck together for survival but wanted nothing to do with the rest of the world.

The barn was used for storage, and, by the smell of it, animals when storms weren't inbound.

She knew she should continue. Only a few more miles. She could get help among the commune. Surely they'd have a phone, wouldn't they?

But the bedding of hay in the loft felt so comfortable against her sore, aching body.

She'd been on the move since this morning. Constant running, hiding. She'd seen two of her friends killed.

"Don't stop," she whispered to herself. "Don't stop." She gritted her teeth, trying to will herself to sit up and move again.

Only a few miles to the commune. Only a few more miles...

But a few miles might as well have been a million. Her feet didn't respond. Too cold. She couldn't feel her toes, though she was wiggling them in her boots.

Maddie lay against the straw, her face screwing up. She wanted to cry, but she wanted, even more, to hold back the emotion.

She let out a shuddering breath, every ounce of resolve poured into forcing herself to sit up.

She had to survive. Her dad would die if she didn't. Her father was clinging on to life as his health deteriorated but had come here to

Nome for her sake. To give her family and her—in his words—*that* kind of money.

The money his relatives had. Maddie wasn't as impressed, but she hadn't refused when they'd enrolled her in St. Andrews, plopping her right at the front of the two-year waiting list. What did she care? She spent most of her nights with her father or praying that he might live a few more months.

If she was hurt, though... if she didn't make it back...

It would break his heart. It would kill him as sure as a gunshot.

Then again... if she died first... Would it be so bad?

"Don't stop," she murmured, growling to herself. In sheer exertion of will, she forced herself into a sitting position, breathing heavily. Her legs dangled over the loft, and she stared across the straw scattered ground. The whole place smelled putrid.

A smell that was somewhat familiar, in fact... She wrinkled her nose, trying to remember where she'd detected that same odor.

She shivered now, rubbing at her arms. And then finally, she sat up.

And then the barn door opened. Slowly, with a soft *creaking* sound.

"Hello?" a voice called into the dark. A voice she recognized. Jasmine's. But Jasmine was dead, and fear now probed up her spine. She held her tongue, frozen in place, refusing to move, her heart pounding wildly.

"Hello? Is anyone in there? Haven't lost your voices again, have you?" A chuckle now. Jasmine's voice switched again, and a gruffer, male voice muttered now, "Dumb kids." He pushed the door open with a muddy foot, looking inside.

Maddie kept low, hiding behind the straw. The man was little more than a silhouette in the dark. She didn't recognize him, not that there was much visible to recognize. She shivered and desperately tried to prevent her teeth from chattering, her heart pounding so wildly, she thought for sure he might hear it.

As he leaned into the barn, looking about in the straw and animal stalls, she felt prickles up her back, and began to move ever so slowly away. But as she did, small bits of hay tumbled through the gaps in the boards under her, meandering down like fluff.

The man looked over, going suddenly still.

So did Maddie, still watching him through the thin, inch-long gap in the hay bales. The hay was old and rotten, though. It smelled of mildew.

Whatever animal was kept in *this* barn, she realized, wasn't a horse or a cow. Now that this horrible thought crossed her mind, she found herself glancing around, looking at the boards nailed to the walls. She shivered as she studied them, staring at marks in the wood.

Some of the wooden boards, towards the base of the barn, had been reinforced. Multiple planks nailed across the openings. Other boards had been cracked or smashed.

The man came to a halt next to one damaged plank of wood. Leaning low, examining it and muttering darkly.

He shook his head, grunted as he moved over to a water barrel, and rolled it to block the opening in the wood. He leaned back now, massaging his neck and letting out a long breath.

Maddie's eyes strained, and she tried to make out the man's face—maybe, if she got to the commune, she could describe him to the police. Then again, she didn't know if the off-gridders had phones.

Worse... she didn't know if this guy was *from* the off-grid commune.

This thought sent another prickle down her back, as she found herself breathing far, far too loudly. In, out. A gusting wind to match the rising gale. Straw fluttered under her lips, and she shifted further back again.

One of the boards creaked.

She froze.

The man's eyes snapped up, fixating on her hiding spot. There was something distinctly *odd* about the man's gaze. No pupils...

How was that possible? Pure black eyes stared up at her. She stared back, frozen in place, shuddering. The man blinked a couple of times, confirming his eyes had no pupils. But then he looked away, and began moving, searching about *under* the loft she'd hidden in.

He moved about under her, murmuring to himself, shifting items about, searching in the dark... Searching for... for what?

For her, she realized with a horrible shudder.

Other realizations whirred through her mind. *Who* was this? Why were his eyes dark? She'd never seen someone without pupils before... an eye condition? Had it been a trick of the light...

Or were the others right?

She'd thought they'd been so silly, talking about the Mockingbird. A story made up only four years ago. She'd done some of her own research, looking online. The blog articles, the small postings on the forums where some of the St. Andrews students hung out, had all whispered about the Mockingbird. Just a joke, she'd thought.

A silly, harmless story. A horror story meant to entertain.

But she'd seen the monster. Had seen it charge towards the cabin. Had heard the roaring. The beast was too large... and now this man... If he was a man. His eyes black...

She pinched herself, wrinkling her nose and shaking her head. *Snap out of it,* she thought firmly. The few-mile trek through the snow had restored some of her sanity. Of course, there were no such things as mythical monsters in the mountains.

This was a man. A man had hunted and killed her friends. The eyes... the monster she'd seen... She didn't know how to explain it all, but she knew there *had* to be some rational explanation.

And either way, whatever this man was, he hadn't seen her.

In a way, his ignorance gave her confidence.

It was like watching the boogeyman bleed.

He was still grunting below her, shifting things about and cursing. "Come on... where are you?" he muttered to himself. And now he was using Terry's voice. Another one of her friends. She'd always pitied Terry. Been scared of him, even. But she knew the others could be downright cruel to the older, taller boy.

She'd never participated in the teasing or gossip behind his back. Though now, shivering in the dark, terrified she would be discovered, she wondered if she could have done more to be kinder to the teenager.

She was determined now, if she escaped, she'd try and make friends with him. Even if he sometimes gave her the creeps.

A sudden groan of wood.

Maddie froze.

Another groan. And she realized now the man was clambering up the ladder to the loft.

She inhaled sharply through her nose and winced. A sudden irritation in her nostrils, something in the air, lingering from the straw.

Another creaking sound. She spotted the top of a head emerging over the edge of the loft. With a faint exhalation, holding back a sneeze, she scampered back, on her hands, sticking to the straw, hoping it would muffle her movements. As she did, the hay fell through gaps in the floor, spinning in clumps towards the ground below.

But the man on the ladder must not have seen as he was already too high up. Or perhaps because his dark eyes were less capable of seeing in the dark.

Whatever the case, she scampered back behind another set of hay bales. Off to her left, there was a gap in the floor. When she peeked through it, though, it only led to a small stall, fenced-in with a muddy floor. And *muddy* was a generous assessment.

She glanced through the gap. A very narrow space. Half a shattered plank of wood. Just big enough for her to slip through? No... no. Too many rusted nails. She winced, imagining the nails tearing through her soft skin. No... no, just stay here. Stay quiet. She nodded, trying to soothe herself.

She peered around her newest hiding spot. The two hay bales by the ladder had served as her initial barrier. And now this single, solitary cover served as her last line of defense. He would check behind it, wouldn't he?

He had to... yes, he would. He'd searched thoroughly downstairs, hadn't he? He'd search here too. Dammit.

She froze, listening as the mountain moaned some more. Flecks of snow flurried through gaps in the barn, speckling her face. The touch of wind assuaged her cheeks, brushed her hair. And then the man pulled himself into the loft.

She caught another glimpse of those eyes but didn't stare long. If she could see his eyes, it meant he could see her.

But again, she felt as if somehow he couldn't see *as* well. As if somehow his strangely darkened eyes were less capable of vision. Was he wearing some strange contacts? It didn't seem so...

She ducked again.

Huffing, as the man drew breath. The sound of boots on the ground, scraping through the hay. A creak of a floorboard. Another step.

"Anybody home?" Jasmine's voice called out in a singsong tone.

He was very good at that, whoever he was. Mimicking voices. Impress ions... that's all it was. An impressionist. She nodded to herself fiercely, determined to tear down the monument of fear attempting to rise in her mind.

This was just an impressionist. Nothing more. She wouldn't give her subconscious the satisfaction of fearing anything further.

"No one at all?" Terry's voice.

"Please, help me." Susan's voice. It finished with Carrie's. "Please... please don't hurt me. I want my daddy."

Chills now, again probing down her spine. Susan was dead. Jasmine was dead. Carrie was dead. Did that mean Terry was dead too?

"Are you back here, little one?" said the dark voice. Another creak. The shadow of the man stretched past the hay bale. She shivered, wedged behind it. Certain he would check. There was nowhere else for him to look. No other hiding spots.

She grit her teeth, tensed, and then made a quick decision.

"Have you found your voices?" the man snapped now, in his own gruff tone. And then he surged forward, grabbing the hay bale she was hiding behind. His fingers clawed into the stuff, ripping tufts and sending them scattering. He cursed, snatched the twine wrapped around the moldy straw and hefted it with a growl, flinging it with a great show of strength across the loft.

Maddie was no longer there.

She seethed, hitting the ground below with a faint *squishing* sound, her ankle nearly buckling from the ten-foot drop. She went still in the stall below, touching her fingers against her side. Sharp, rusted nails had scraped against her flank, drawing blood. But she'd slipped through the broken floorboard and now stared up from where she crouched in the dark, in the mucky stall, inhaling a putrid stench.

A shadow passed over the gap above her. And then a string of expletives descended, wafting towards her. "I guess no one's home... oh well..."

She heard a *thump,* and realized with horror, he'd jumped down from the loft, landing in front of her. He took a couple of stumbling footsteps, regaining his balance by catching a support beam in the middle of the barn.

He shot a final look through the stalls, and Maddie closed her eyes, though, she hated doing it—she didn't want any reflection to snare his attention.

She heard a faint gasp and opened her eyes again in time to watch the man turn and move away. He had something in his hand now. A small packet of something. He ripped it and was whistling now. A strange, long whistle followed by a throaty clicking sound.

Similar sounds she'd heard hunters make, attempting to draw specific types of prey.

The man stood in the door of the barn now, and he waved the item in his hand about, blowing on it a bit. And then tossing it over his shoulder. "Come on, big guy! Leave it alone—he's dead."

Maddie felt her heart skip. *Dead*? Someone else was dead...

The man by the door kept wafting with his hand, as if fanning flames, over the small packet he'd ripped. "Smell that, big guy? Yeah—it's nice, isn't it."

Maddie didn't know who he was talking to, but shivering in the back stall, amidst the muck, she felt a slow, rising sense of relief. He wasn't looking at her with those demon eyes of his. Wasn't speaking to her at all—had decided no one was in the barn.

Lucky. She'd known she'd been lucky. But sometimes a girl needed all the luck she could get. She stared towards the figure in the door, still waving his palm back and forth while emitting that clicking sound.

A few seconds passed... and then she heard a growl.

Maddie stared... a dark shape was lumbering through the snow, moving towards them... A large shape. Not a black bear. Not a grizzly.

"Come on, big guy—I'm gonna need you for later. Yeah, there you are—smell that? Hmm?" The man by the door stepped back hurriedly, kicking the ripped packet in the doorway further into the barn.

It landed only ten feet from Maddie's stall.

The large, lumbering shape had to be at least two tons of muscle and blubber. It was growling, steam rising out of its nostrils. The beast slipped through the barn door with practiced ease, as if it had done so many times before.

The silhouette of the man gave it a wide berth, cackling as he did. "There you go. Just sit still for a bit, okay. What's that you're gnawing on? Oh—shit—okay, no... no, that's all yours."

The monster stopped in the middle of the barn, huffing and snuffling, and pausing over the packet on the ground, inhaling it.

And now, Maddie detected the odor. A strong, powerful stink that wafted towards her. She wrinkled her nose, her eyes stinging nearly instantly. She recognized that smell. The same odor back at camp.

The man by the doors slipped behind the monster, out into the snow. He shut the doors. There was a loud *creak,* suggesting the wooden bar was lowered into place.

And then Maddie was once more sealed in the dark, like a skeleton in a tomb.

But this time, she had company.

She could hear it. The growling, the sniffing. The low grumble in the monster's throat. But she could no longer see it.

Her breath came quickly. He'd locked her in the barn with his monster.

And by the sound of things, the creature was coming closer.

CHAPTER 14

ELLA KEPT AN EYE on Priscilla and the rest of the party, but it was Brenner's voice that caused her to veer off.

She spotted the marshal, waving to her from up the slope, calling out. "Up here—Ella, is that you? I found something."

Ella hesitated, glancing after her sister. "Priscilla!" she called out. "Brenner found something."

But a chorus of voices drowned out Ella's cry. "Maddie? James! Carrie!" The voices carried on the night, caught in the wind. The snow was falling fast. The blizzard was already here, and it would only intensify as the worst of the storm settled.

They needed to get off the mountain.

"Priscilla! Brenner found something!" Ella shouted.

Priscilla half-turned, still moving as she did, glancing back towards her sister. "Hurry up!" Cilla called. "Hurry!"

Ella huffed in frustration. Brenner was still waving her over. She glanced after her sister, and the other search members, who all had lights now, flashing through the snow. They moved in a straggling line, up the slope, past more orange flags, desperately searching.

Brenner was gesturing towards her. Priscilla had finally spotted the source of Ella's attention. But then another voice. "Help!"

Coming from off near the base of a cliff. "Please—please, any-one—help me!"

Priscilla whirled about. Some of her police officers hastened forward as well, lights joining together into one large spotlight, illuminating the base of the small gully.

Ella didn't recognize the voice. A male voice?

"Who is that?" Priscilla shouted.

"James! Please—are you—you police? Please! Help me! I'm thirsty!"

Priscilla let out a shout of triumph. "Go—go, grab him!" she yelled at the others. "There—no—down that way. You morons, get out of the way." Ella watched as Priscilla did it herself, reaching out to snatch at a hand and using it to lower herself onto handholds in the rock, which led down the twenty-foot drop towards where the voice was emanating from.

Ella peered over and thought she spotted a thin, dark figure waving up at them. Flashlights caught a handsome, dark-skinned face.

James.

Ella released a breath in relief. She watched as Priscilla, indifferent to her own safety, stubbornly clambered down the rocks, occasionally slipping but catching herself as she descended towards the desperate figure. His movements were slow, his words slurred. He looked exhausted.

Ella turned, glancing towards where Brenner was still waving her over. He stood between some trees, a grim look on his face, his hand resting on his firearm. The expressions of gladness and triumph over the search party's visages were *not* mirrored in the marshal's grim countenance.

Ella tugged at the arm of a cop. "Hey, hey, we're just up there. Alright?"

The cop glanced at her, sweaty-faced despite the snow. He blinked a few times, wincing. He had pinched features and was wearing snow-goggles. "Umm... alright. I'll come with Agent Porter."

"Oh, no, that's fine."

But he shook his head determinedly. "No splitting up. Chief's orders."

Ella smiled, nodding in gratitude. She waited a few seconds as the man reported to his superior, pointing off with a gloved hand towards Brenner's tree line, and then he hurried over, moving next to Ella. "Alright—just this way?"

She nodded. "Thank you."

"No worries. I'm Ralph Thompson."

"T-thompson? As in..."

He nodded once, tight-lipped. "Susan's brother. Yup."

"I'm so sorry for your loss—"

"Thanks. It's fine. Here—just up that way..."

He led her up the slope towards Brenner, his curt response clearly indicating he had no interest in speaking of his sister, the first victim. But Ella didn't blame him and didn't press the point. If anything, she admired that he was still out on the mountain.

Brenner stood leaning against one of the trees, watching them approach with a deepening frown. The curving switchback moved up the bluff, outlined with small red flags. Ella's own flashlight swished across the ground, illuminating flurries of snow, and the shadows from the snowflakes like dark fireflies agitated against the trail.

Brenner was moving again, gesturing at them. "I found another," he said, his eyes grim.

Ella felt her heart skip. Ralph Thompson moved behind her, keeping pace, his hand resting on his belt. She shot a look back towards him, and he frowned off to the side, staring at the ground. "The commune isn't far from here," Ralph said softly.

"What was that?" Ella asked, turning her head but continuing her movement up the trail, curving around the bend, and now approaching where Brenner waited.

"I said the commune isn't far from here," Ralph repeated, louder now. "You know—the self-sustaining types. They're up this way. Hunting, planting what they can, living together. I hear the leader there sleeps with nine different women." He shrugged. "Interesting place."

Ella nodded, breathing heavily. "You know much about them?"

"Nah. Susan was interested at one point. That leader of theirs... he's like forty—Susan is..." he coughed, clearing his throat.

Ella stood there, shivering, momentarily forgetting Brenner. Momentarily forgetting the others pulling James from the gully. In that brief moment, the only two people in the world now faced each other in the snow. Ella a few paces higher, elevated. She was a small woman, though, *petite* some said. *Shorty,* Brenner used to tease. And so she wasn't any taller than the man, even though he was about half a foot lower than her.

"Your sister was interested in this commune, then?"

"Yeah. She told me," he said, disgustedly. "But couldn't join until she turned eighteen. But that was gonna be next week. She was gonna join them. Or at least try."

"And how did you take that news?"

"What?" He hesitated then scowled. "Are you asking me if I did this?"

"No. That's not what I said."

The snow was flurrying. The wind screeching. She had to raise her voice to be heard. She could feel Brenner watching them both. She tried a different tack, pulling on threads now. She didn't know *what* the threads led to, nor what would unwind by her pulling. But she knew, now, that the best thing to do was check every lead.

Zeke Chernow had tried to kill Aspen O'Connor. He had bear bait on him.

But he *hadn't* killed Susan. Maybe not Jasmine. Ella said, "Any reason Zeke Chernow might have wanted to hurt your sister?"

"What? Oh—Zeke. I saw your sister shoot him. Rough, that."

He was puffing air, sending snow off his thin upper lip and his pinched face.

"You didn't answer my question."

"No. I guess I didn't. I mean, it's obvious isn't it?"

"What is?" She hesitated, then called back, "One second, Brenner." She returned her attention to Susan's brother.

The cop shrugged, a fur collar rising against his chin. "Zeke *Chernow.*"

"Carrie's father, I know."

"What... no... *Chernow.* Remember? Like four years ago. Wait, shit. I forgot. You weren't here then."

He hadn't meant it to sound like an accusation, but Ella took it as one.

"What happened four years ago?"

"Zeke's kid. They killed him."

Ella just stared. "I... what? Why's this the first I'm hearing about it. None of the kids had a criminal record."

"No, not like that. I mean, the bastard deserved to die. Susan did the right thing. I guess. I mean, I'm still pissed she went and died. Wanted to leave us, but..." he trailed off, swallowing, his face red now. He tugged at the corners of his hood, pulling it forward.

Ella had lost track of Brenner now. He'd turned to head back into the tree line again.

But she was too focused to follow. "These teenagers killed someone... what do you mean?"

"I mean he was threatening to do some messed up stuff at that school. About four years ago. They were all new. Youngsters. The school has an eighth grade. Goes eighth through twelfth. Zeke's oldest was a senior. Woulda been twenty back then. But he was trouble."

"What type of trouble?"

"Harassing some of the teachers. Writing threatening letters. Turned out that he once let a raccoon into the principal's office..."

"That's not so bad."

"Raccoon had rabies, and Zeke's kid knew it."

"I don't get where your sister comes into this."

"There was an event... umm... it was messed up. You know, maybe I should mention, I went to the same school. I was in the same grade as Jason."

"Jason is the one who died?"

"Zeke's son, yeah. But... well, he killed *himself,* but in his suicide letter, he blamed them."

Ella shivered, blowing air through her lips just to warm them. She tilted her shoulder as if to stave off the worst of the flailing winter.

"So you went to St. Andrew's as well?"

"I mean, a lot of us do. Especially with, you know, our parents. Th ompsons... right? Thompsons' Fishing? Anyway, whatever. He sent Susan and me there. We actually spent time at each other's houses a bunch."

He gave a quick shrug. Ella nibbled on her lip. She could tell he was being evasive now. She hesitated a second longer, then said softly. "So what happened with Jason?"

"There was a party. Someone got drunk. Accused Jason of attacking them. He denied it. But then some of the younger students came forward. Said they saw him do it—saw him attack this girl on the beach."

"What was the girl's name?"

"I dunno. She moved away from Nome, though."

"Alright. So let me guess... The kids who accused Zeke's son... your sister?"

He nodded

"James?"

Another nod. "All of them were there. Except for your cousin. Madison. But the rest of them. They said they witnessed the attack."

"What about Terry?"

"Yeah... I mean, just so we're clear I mentioned this to Chief Baker, but he said it had nothing to do with the case. Terry... Terry was dealing then already. Small time stuff, but he was the friendliest with Jason. Jason used to tell Terry these wild stories and stuff."

"Stories?"

"Yeah... dunno much about it."

Ella frowned now, feeling a surge of frustration. She shot a look down the slope towards where James Bender had been recovered up the cliff and was being hastily bundled and escorted by two cops back down the mountain. Priscilla was pressing on, refusing to take a moment's respite.

Ella watched her sister trudge through the snow, head down, golden locks billowing behind her.

Ella turned her attention once again to the young cop. "So what happened after?"

"I... I dunno, really."

"You said they killed Jason Chernow."

"No... I mean, yes. They led to him killing himself. Because they wouldn't let it go."

"You sound sympathetic to Jason."

He scratched at his chin, shaking his head and letting out a breath. "Yeah... I mean, you know—we used to be friends. I guess I feel bad for the guy. His own dad and sister found him hanging in his cabin. It was this whole thing."

Ella paused, shaking her head. "How come the Chernows were allowed at St. Andrew's? Mr. Chernow isn't exactly loaded."

A scoff. "He used to be. His old man was one of the original prospectors. A real old-timer. Made millions. But the guy was smart. Put the money in a trust fund for his grandbabies, where the drunk couldn't get to it."

"So the kids had money, but Zeke didn't?"

"That's right."

Ella hesitated. She then said, her voice carrying a would-be innocent lilt, "Any reason you can think why Chief Baker wouldn't mention this to me?"

He shrugged. "Hey... you know what. Looks like the others are heading out. Maybe... maybe you got it from here on your own, yeah?"

She frowned at him but gave a quick nod. "Yeah... maybe."

Thompson shifted. He paused, looking back up at her, and opened his mouth. Then let out a sigh, turning again. But he paused again, as if thinking better of it, and whirled around. He blurted out, "You're Fed, right? You should check out that commune."

"Why?"

"Because," he said, his voice bitter. "That bastard was trying to get with my sister. He should be..." Thompson trailed off, gritting his teeth and huffing air through tight teeth. He shrugged.

Ella watched as Thompson turned and moved away. She stood there for a moment, frowning, trying to make sense of what she'd just heard.

The man clearly had wanted to tell her this last part... maybe all of it.

She frowned as he retreated, joining the search party. But instead of veering off and following Priscilla through the snow, the young cop turned and followed the three figures stumbling back towards base camp. James, the survivor, and the two cops on either side. Thompson's gloved thumbs were still hooked in his belt, his right hand bumping against his holster, his shoulders hunched.

Ella watched him go, feeling a tug in her gut.

Too many angles now... Too much information. She was trying to focus on the details but was having a hard time finding out *which* details to pay attention to. The commune? Perhaps... or just a personal vendetta of Thompson's. If everyone was of legal age and consensual, as much as it bothered Thompson, there wasn't much she could do about it.

She turned now, her face still stinging, blinking snowflakes from her eyelashes. Brenner was hunched by something in the snow, and she moved under the trees now, granted respite from the worst of the wind and the snow. The boughs above her were thick with frost, though, blocking out any interruption of the ambiance from the moon beyond the clouds.

The only light came from her flashlight and Brenner's.

As she approached from behind, she tried to catalogue the information she'd been given.

On one hand, Terry Havek had said something that stuck with her. James Bender had said Terry smelled too much, so he had left the tent.

But what if that stench wasn't the smell of Terry's skunk weed but, rather, the same smell Ella had found in Zeke's bait bag? The same bait he'd had in his pocket. The stench had been incredible, but she supposed it had to be in order to attract bears.

This mattered. The best explanation for what had attacked the campsite was clearly a bear. But a person too. Bears couldn't tie someone to a tree. However... kids knew what a *bear* was, so how come they called it a monster?

If not a bear, then what? So a man, with the help of *something*... as wild as it sounded... had attacked the campsite.

This was confirmed. Zeke was not the killer. This was also confirmed.

Zeke's son had committed suicide according to Thompson. So Zeke had motive, had tried to attack Aspen... Had Zeke hired someone, then? Maybe a friend? An assassin?

Ella shivered, remembering the gunshots. The same assassin who'd come after her?

And what about the two remaining missing girls? Madison Porter and Carrie Chernow.

Carrie... what if Carrie was involved? Helping her father?

But Ella shook her head. It was possible. Did that explain the footstep in the blood where Jasmine had been found? A small footstep, of a young woman. Maybe Carrie Chernow was avenging her brother. Helping her father...

They hadn't found Carrie's corpse. Or the girl herself.

Ella considered this a moment but then shook her head. Carrie was a friend of these teenagers. If she'd resented them, how had she been so close with them, for years? According to Thompson, *Carrie* had testified against her own brother.

So no... if not Carrie then... Back to Zeke.

It was the only thing that made sense. Zeke Chernow had means, motive and...

No opportunity.

Ella huffed in frustration and came to a halt next to Brenner.

He was pointing at something in the snow, and Ella stared down. She went still, eyes wide. A bloody jacket. And then, Brenner pointed up, over a sharp drop-off along the cliff.

Ella stared, wincing. A body in the trees.

A young woman, moving with the faint shift and sway of the branches, her head arched back, her arms splayed out. Motionless, half covered in snow.

"Carrie Chernow," Brenner said quietly. "I can't get to her. Too steep."

Ella stared at the corpse, her heart in her throat. So there went that theory. Carrie wasn't helping her father. Zeke had an alibi—and was dead.

So he must have hired someone. But who would take a job like this? And why couldn't she find them?

Her teeth chattered, and she looked away from the body in the tree. "We can't reach it?" she said.

"No. Tried for like twenty minutes. Gotta wait for the blizzard to pass."

"Blizzard will cover everything."

Brenner paused, then pulled a knife from his belt in a quick motion. He jammed it through the jacket, pinning the bloody fabric to the trees.

"Should we call it in?"

Brenner nodded. "Needed the SAT phone. You got it?"

Ella shivered, nodding and removing the device from her pocket as she did. Her fingers brushed her own smartphone. She hadn't checked this in some time. Reception was nearly non-existent in the mountains after all.

She stared through the night, frowning. As she pulled the satellite phone, she also noticed her own phone's notification light blinking white.

A message.

Dread filled her. The same dread now accompanying the motion of the body in the trees. She shivered, removed the phone slowly, and read the newest message.

Arrived. Where can I meet you?

She cursed beneath her breath, her gloved hand tightening around her phone. She resisted the urge to hurl it against the tree.

"What's wrong?" Brenner said.

"N-nothing. Umm. It's fine."

He watched her with that accusing gaze of his, but he was too tired to say anything. He kept looking up at the body in the trees, over the cliff. Too far down to reach. The pass now blocked with snow. They'd have to wait. The bloody jacket shook and swayed on the tree, pinned by his knife. It would have to serve as a marker.

Ella hastily stowed her phone without answering. Arrived. He was here. The Graveyard Killer was in Nome.

What was she supposed to do about it?

"You okay?" Brenner said.

"Are you?" she shot back.

"No."

"Me neither."

They both went quiet. Ella shook her head, her bangs wet now against her forehead, under her hood. She shot a look down the trail, frowning. "What do you know about Thompson?"

"Who? Oh, Ralph?"

"Yeah."

"Yeah, damn. Forgot he was up here. How was he? You know... Susan?" Brenner stared at her, a look of concern in his eyes.

Ella shook her head. "I don't know. He seemed off."

"Off how?"

She shrugged.

"Wait, you don't think Ralph is involved, do you?"

"No... no. I'm just trying to figure out why Zeke attacked Aspen."

"Wait, what the hell?"

She nodded grimly, leaning against the tree, turning to avoid having the body in her line of sight. She hesitated briefly, marking the coordinates on the SAT phone to help the coroner find the body later. Then sent a text to Baker's number. *Found Carrie. Dead.*

She lowered the phone, grim.

Only Maddie Porter left.

The others were either dead or rescued. Three of them so far... Susan, Jasmine and Carrie. Killed.

But by who?

Brenner was leaning forward now, frowning. "You're serious? Is Aspen alive?"

"We found her a bit ago. Yeah. She's fine. Cilla shot him."

"Zeke? Is he—"

"Dead."

"So it was him... he did this?" Brenner looked with horror at Carrie's body. "To his own daughter? That demonic little—"

"I don't think Zeke killed her."

"Why not?"

"His parole officer said he met with Zeke earlier. The same time Susan was attacked? Two hours away."

Brenner scratched at his face. "But you saw Zeke go after Aspen?"

"Yeah. And get this. With bear bait in his pocket. His own bear bait, by the look of it—homemade."

"Bear bait... so it was him. He set a bear on the camp and then killed Susan. Hunted the others, then followed them up the mountain, attacking them. Even his own daughter—the sick freak."

"No," Ella said. "He couldn't have. He was in town at the time of the first murder. Two hours away."

"Says the parole officer? Have you looked into that guy?"

Ella hesitated; blinked. "Oh. Umm... No?"

"Well, there you go. There's your accomplice. He's covering for Zeke."

"Why, though? Why would he?"

"Who the hell knows? But it's him. What was his name again?"

Ella hesitated, shaking her head. She then said, "I... I know we need to keep looking for Maddie. And I will." She paused as another gust of wind, carrying snow even through the trees, squealed by. She then said, over the gale, "But I want to go check on James. See if he can talk. He might be able to tell us where Maddie is."

"Plus? What else. You look scared."

"I'm... no. I just... I want to make sure Thompson is playing nice."

"So he was acting super odd, huh?"

"And by the sound of things, he was a friend of Jason Chernow. The kid who committed suicide. Zeke's son."

Brenner fell into step next to her. "Yeah, I remember that. About four years ago."

"Four years... That's about the time those stories about the Mockingbird arose, right?"

"Huh... I guess so. You think that's part of this?"

"Definitely part of it. I don't have a clue how."

"You think the monster is real?"

"No. I mean... yes. But not a supernatural monster. Just a run-of-the-mill type."

"It's Zeke. Him and his parole officer. Hell, maybe Ralph Thompson too."

"Ralph related to any PO's?" Ella asked.

Brenner hesitated as he moved next to her, thinking, but then shook his head. "Nah. Rich family. He's the only cop."

Ella sighed. "I... let's find Thompson. Then I want to look something up."

Brenner just gestured for her to lead the way.

Ella broke into a jog. She moved through the snow, slipping and nearly stumbling as she did. But Priscilla's accusations rang in her ears.

Was it true that Ella didn't care about family? She cared more about catching a bad guy than Maddie?

No... No, she didn't believe that. Ella didn't know *where* Maddie was. But the best way to find her cousin, she decided, was to speak with James Bender. Aspen too, if she had the chance. The blizzard was now swelling around them. Maddie would either be in shelter or... like the three other girls...

Ella winced, jogging faster now, muttering a small prayer under her breath, if only to absolve her conscience, and then hurrying down the slopes with Brenner moving closely behind.

CHAPTER 15

Ella exhaled deeply, standing in the portable floodlights brought up to illuminate base camp. Bright, glowing lights settled amidst the trees, like the glare of a football stadium. And Ella watched where Thompson slipped into a car and drove back down the mountain.

By the look of things, James Bender was still sitting in the back of a police car. Next to Terry Havek. And, to her surprise, in the front seat, Aspen O'Connor.

The three kids were looking nervously towards where Chief Baker was speaking animatedly with Aspen's mother.

"You heard her, Candace," Baker was saying. "They need to be taken in for observation. They've been out here for hours. Who knows what they're suffering from."

Mrs. O'Connor was shaking her head, furious. "My daughter isn't a liar, Chief! If she says she saw the Mockingbird, then she did!"

But Chief Baker just flung his hands up in exhaustion. "Have it your way. Follow if you want. But I'm leaving. Now!"

O'Connor protested a bit more, but Chief Baker pointed determinedly towards the woman's car. She glared, but then decided to obey, moving hastily towards her SUV, the headlights already on, suggesting the engine was running. The woman moved in slow, delicate steps, avoiding a nasty fall on the slick ground.

Ella watched as Baker moved around the front of the SUV, hesitating. Then she said, "One sec, Brenner. Be right back."

Brenner nodded, watching where Thompson disappeared down the road. Susan's brother, the young cop, was no longer lingering near the campers. Ella wondered if this meant he wasn't involved after all, or—perhaps—if he was going to lay an ambush at the base of the mountain.

She shook her head. This whole business was making her paranoid.

She moved swiftly through the rising snow, which now crunched beneath her boots, as she marched up to Chief Baker. He was cursing as he tried to shove open his door, sweeping it across the frost, scowling as he did. "Damn thing..." the man growled, shaking his head, his impressive mustache now streaked with snow.

He managed to push the door open against the snowbank with a scraping sound and began to slide into the front seat.

His was one of the few remaining vehicles. The others all belonged to the police by the look of them. A small tent had been set up around Zeke Chernow's body, preserving it for the coroner when the blizzard passed.

Carrie's body would also be recovered when the storm abated.

Ella raised a hand. "Baker!" she called.

He scowled at her, peering over the roof. "Cilla?"

Ella felt distinctly uncomfortable and shook her head adamantly. "Ella!" she retorted.

"Oh." He looked embarrassed. "What is it? Is Cilla back yet?"

Ella shook her head. "I think she's still searching."

"God damn that woman," Baker said, then winced, glanced at the teenagers in the car, and slammed the door, rolling his shoulders in his thick jacket. "Well, you and Gunn better get going too."

Ella held up a finger. She winced. "Can I... please, speak with them for a second?"

She pointed through the window.

Baker frowned. "Now hang on a moment..."

"Just a second."

Baker shook his head. "We're leaving Ella!" He opened the door again with another loud scraping sound."

"Fine!" she exclaimed. "That's fine. I'll come with!"

"Suit yourself. Tell Brenner to get moving too. This is just the start. It's going to be a bad one. Worst blizzard in ten years they say. God damn that woman..." he added again, quieter now and staring up the slope where his wife had led the cops.

Ella fidgeted uncomfortably. She felt a flash of... guilt.

She wondered what it would feel like to have someone who cared that much about her. She never had... had she? Not her parents, her family. She didn't really date, other than casually. She'd never been married. Almost thirty now and counting.

She shook her head, frowning. Sky-diving, paragliding, spelunking... the sorts of adventures she enjoyed. She was even on track to get her pilot's license. Ella might have looked like Cinderella to some, but others knew her as an adrenaline junkie. By sheer acts of will, she forced herself to do things others wouldn't in order to solve the case.

And now... now in order to rescue family, too.

Cilla was doing the same thing.

And Ella found she grudgingly respected her sister for it.

She hurried around the car, opened the back door and slid in next to Terry Havek. The large kid, who was still in cuffs, glanced at her, smiling from under his dark fringe. She smiled back. Baker gunned the engine and began moving down the slope, slowly. Further away from the mountain, away from the killer in the snow, and away from Maddie Porter.

In the opposite direction Ella wanted to go.

So she spoke quickly. "Guys, sorry, but I need to hear what you saw."

The three survivors were glancing at her in the rearview mirror, all of them nervous. James Bender leaned against the door, his eyes closed as if nearly asleep. Aspen was in the front seat, shifting uncomfortably. Terry stared at her enraptured, as if he'd caught sight of an angel.

"Please," Ella said.

Baker had turned on the music, and she scowled at him. He turned it up.

She shook her head in frustration as the man, listening to some old-timer country tunes, began trundling down the mountain.

"I need to know about the Mockingbird. You say you saw it?"

They all looked at her sheepishly, hesitant. Aspen glanced at James. James' eyes were still closed. Terry nodded adamantly. "Yeah—that's what it was. The Mockingbird! It's the best explanation. I've been thinking. That's what I saw. Like I said—I saw this big—"

"Really big," Aspen added. "Monster. It was like a ghost."

"No it wasn't," James whispered. "It just had white fur."

"White fur," Terry said. "That's the Mockingbird's appearance when he steals your voice."

"What do you mean?" Ella asked. "Steal your voice?" She remembered what Zeke had muttered before attacking Aspen. *Found their voices... Found their voices...*

She hesitated. "Where did you first hear about the Mockingbird?"

Now that an adult seemed to be taking the car full of late teenagers seriously, they all were watching her. Even James. His eyes were blood-shot, and he looked badly dehydrated. He was still trembling even though the car was warm.

"At school," Aspen and James said together.

Terry nodded.

"From who?" Ella asked.

They all glanced at one another. Aspen pointed at Terry. So did James. Terry scowled. "I didn't make it up!" he snapped.

"Who did?"

He looked guilty all of a sudden, shrugging.

But now everyone, even Chief Baker who'd lowered the music volume to listen in while guiding the vehicle down the slope, stared at him.

"Who did, Terry?" Ella asked.

"Answer her, boy," Baker growled.

And the grumbling voice, like the snarl of a wolf seemed to do it. "Jason," Terry muttered. "Before he killed himself."

"Hung himself," Aspen said, wincing. "Carrie found him... She said it was so horrible. I feel so bad for her... Do we know where Carrie is?" Aspen said suddenly, her voice rising in hope.

Ella noticed there was no mention of Zeke. And Ella didn't have the heart to tell these survivors what had happened to their friend. So instead, she focused on Terry.

"So Jason told you the tale, is that right? He talked about the Mockingbird a lot?"

"Yeah," said Aspen. "I heard him tell it too, but Terry also told me. Terry really liked the stories," she said slowly, giving the young man a long look. Then, quickly, she said, "Why is Terry in cuffs?"

"I didn't really like the stories," Terry shot back. "I just thought they were interesting. Jason told them funny, like an audiobook, you know. Doing the voices and everything. When I was... er, delivering him pizzas at times. I felt bad for him, you know. And I don't think he knew I was gonna testify against him. I sure as hell didn't tell him. Just delivered the stuff I was delivering and hung out a bit. I mean... he wasn't *so* bad, you know."

"He was awful," Aspen snapped.

"Yeah, yeah, awful," Terry agreed quickly, nodding sheepishly.

Ella frowned. "What do you mean doing the voices?"

Terry glanced at her. "I mean... Jason was really good at voices. He wanted to be an impressionist. He worked really hard at it."

Ella tensed, leaning back in her seat, shaking her head. "And so what happened to Jason, then? I heard you three testified against him for an attempted assault."

All three teens nodded slowly now. Aspen frowned. "They tried to threaten us not to."

Baker cleared his throat. "I mean, I wouldn't say anyone was *threatened.*"

But Ella cut in. "Threatened how?"

"They told us not to talk. Bunch of lawyers in Jason's grandpa's trust offered us money, but we told them to go to hell."

James smiled, nodding. "Aspen came up with the slogan."

"What slogan?" Ella said quietly.

"You can't steal our voices," Terry said. "So we all did testify, you know. Or we would've but then... Jason killed himself so there was no point."

Ella felt the morbid weight of the moment settle on her. She shivered, shaking her head. She frowned at Chief Baker, though. She shifted a bit, moving so she could lean past Terry Havek's cuffed form. And she met Chief Baker's eyes in the rearview mirror.

"So Jason made up this story... And he was good at impressions. Did that trait run in the family?"

"What are you asking?" asked Baker, frowning back.

"Did Zeke do impressions? He made bear bait. Seemed eccentric. Would he do voices like his son?"

Baker shrugged. "Dunno. Why?"

"What do you know about a Parole Officer in Nome named Paolini? Joe Paolini?"

Baker just shook his head. "Good guy. Dunno much, why?" He paused, not listening now as he was forced to slow, cursing as their tires began to slip. But he managed to regain control and returned to crawling down the mountainside, glaring. He kept checking his radio and the small GPS display on his car, likely looking for any replies from his wife. Ella noticed two text messages already sent, displayed by bubbles in the heads-up display. Both to Priscilla. Both reading, *U okay?*

The last one had received a response. A thumbs up. That was it.

Baker's fingers tapped nervously against the steering wheel as he continued down the mountain. Ella watched him from behind, and occasionally glanced at the surviving campers, trying to make sense of it.

The Mockingbird... Zeke Chernow. Jason Chernow's suicide... Parole Officer Paolini being a good guy.

What was she missing?

And then she said suddenly, "Baker, why didn't you tell me about the trial? About the kids pointing the finger at Mr. Chernow?"

"Hmm?"

"I heard from a reliable source that you didn't want me notified about it. Why?"

Baker looked distinctly uncomfortable now. "I don't know what you mean."

Ella watched him. She could feel the others in the car watching as well. She didn't press with anger. Didn't raise her voice. But said, softly, "How did Jason Chernow die?"

"Hung himself," said Baker quickly. "Was found by his father and sister."

"Did the coroner see the body?"

"Of course—what the hell kinda slipshod department do you think I run?"

But Ella was now tapping her fingers against her leg. She said slowly, "If Zeke didn't kill them, because his Parole Officer was telling the truth, then that means someone else did. Someone who might've had access to his father's bear bait. And if he really was good at impressions... maybe that's why he started the Mockingbird myth... It all goes back to Jason, doesn't it?"

"Except one thing," Baker snapped. "Jason Chernow is dead. He was found swinging. The coroner confirmed it. That's it."

"So why didn't you want me to know about the trial?" Ella said firmly once more.

Chief Baker cursed and slammed the brakes. It took a second for them to work, and the car slipped a bit. It slid to the side, biting into a large mound of snow. But Baker didn't care. He flung open his door, marched around the side of the vehicle and flung open Ella's door. He pointed at the snow in front of him, his face beet red. "You wanna talk about my reputation, we do it in private Porter! So come on, what are you asking me?"

Ella hesitated, but then slipped out of the car, standing and facing the man. She frowned at him, and he scowled back. He shut the door behind her with a slam.

And now the two of them stood next to the spun-out vehicle, on the side of the snowy mountain, as a blizzard descended on their shoulders.

Baker had long since lost his temper, but Ella's wick was longer. She kept calm. "What are you so mad about, Matthias?"

"This bullshit—you're interrogating *me*. Me, in front of a suspect!"

"Terry isn't a suspect."

"He kissed a dead girl, Ella!"

"I don't think he knew she was dead."

"Then that's almost as bad. He kissed a tied up girl?"

Ella nodded slowly, but she refused to be distracted. Terry was going to have to face a judge, most likely. But Baker was deflecting. She said, "What don't you want me to know about the Chernow case?"

"What the hell, Ella? Drop it. Nothing."

"Is Jason dead?"

"What?"

"I keep coming back to that. It's the one thing that keeps pinballing in my mind. Is Jason dead? His father and sister found him, you say. But if there's anyone who might lie about a brother's death… to save his reputation. To save him from prison time, it'd be the father and sister. No?"

Baker was shaking his head, snowflakes settling on his crown of dark hair. He smoothed his mustache with his fingers, parts of it frozen. "You don't know what the hell you're talking about."

The two of them were cast as silhouettes across the snow bank by the car's bright lights.

Ella was shivering again, but she didn't look away, studying Baker closely. A theory was brewing in her mind, slowly bubbling up. A theory born of the gold mines in Nome. Born of a lifetime as the sister to Priscilla Porter. She knew the methods of her family. Someone had taken a shot at her on the mountain, and she had a couple of guesses who'd paid the gunman.

But all the roads were leading to one place.

And Baker was acting like a guilty man.

So she went fishing, but this time with strong bait. "Who paid you to hide Jason Chernow's case?"

His eyes bugged. "You're insane."

"You would've hit me if I wasn't right."

"Contrary to your sensibilities, Eleanor," he sneered, "I don't make a habit of striking women. Especially not *family*."

The word stung as he flung it at her. The kids were all watching them closely, staring through the glass windows. Their breath fogged the car.

Ella said slowly. "Here's what I think happened. Jason got in trouble four years ago. He was going to be put away. The teenagers were ready to testify. They had a slogan—about not stealing their voices. Jason made up this whole thing about the Mockingbird. Part sick joke, part scare tactic maybe. He's obsessed with mimicking voices... isn't that what the Mockingbird does?"

"There's no such thing."

"No... There isn't. Only in the minds of them." She nodded towards the car. The bitterly cold air flooding her hood as she moved. She winced and glanced away from the bright lights of the vehicle. "And so someone wanted them scared. Someone wanted them to suffer. Who might that be?"

"I get your point Ella..." Baker hesitated. "But... it's not Jason."

"Because he's dead?"

"It's not him."

"So he isn't dead?"

Baker shook his head, paused. He stared at her, then said, slowly. "If I thought there was a chance that Jason Chernow was behind all of this, I'd tell you, Ella. You might think I'm a shit cop. But I'm not. I care about this job and this department."

"I can see that. But you're not telling me he's dead anymore. Why?"

Baker let out a long puff of air. He turned, looking across the hood of the car, listening to the rumble of the engine, the whine of the wind. Then he looked back at her, holding an arm up, in part to block the flurry of snow, but also, she guessed, as if to shield himself from the witnesses in his own car.

He said, "What do you know? Who have you been talking to? Hmm? Stop playing coy, Ella. You know, don't you?"

She looked at him. Then nodded. "I know," she said. Though she didn't have the slightest suspicion what he meant. Still, she'd gone fishing, and now something was hooked. All she needed to do was slowly reel it in.

Baker sighed. "It wasn't a bribe."

She felt her heart skip. "No. I know it wasn't."

"Who told you?"

"I can't tell you that, Baker."

"Did they tell you that we did it right? By the book? Look... We processed the case. Jason admitted to everything. We sentenced him. Five years. It was clean. The only thing Zeke asked was for me to let him tell the lie, okay? That was it. A small, stupid lie. Just to protect his family's name. That was all."

Ella stared, stunned. "You lied about Jason Chernow's suicide?" This, she guessed, was why Baker hadn't wanted her to look too closely at the trial from four years ago.

But Baker shook his head. "It wasn't like that. Zeke came to me. Said his son would confess. Didn't need the whole trial business. Would cop a plea in front of a judge. Guilty on all charges. We'd send him away for five. Normally, you'd get less than two, by the way," Baker said, his chin jutting out. His tone proud.

"So Jason is in prison right now?"

"Yeah. Down in Seattle. Has been for five years. Zeke and his daughter spread the rumor. Lying about Jason's suicide. You know, the family has been through so much... I didn't want to drag 'em through it. So I didn't counter the point. The newspapers just reported what Zeke said. The judge didn't say a word. Didn't care too. It was over. *Is* over."

Ella gestured at the car. "Three of them are dead, Matthias. It's not over for them."

"This has nothing to do with that!"

"You really think that? The friend group who were going to testify against Jason Chernow is targeted by the Mockingbird. This made-up monster *Jason* came up with. Zeke Chernow attacked Aspen. Had bear bait on him. You don't think it might have a smidgen to do with it?" Ella hesitated, realizing some of her frustration was turning to sarcasm. So she paused, breathed, then murmured. "Sorry. Baker, just tell me where Jason is supposed to be in prison."

"Not supposed to. He's been there four years. He has another year. No possibility of parole."

Ella watched him, and she felt a surge of realization. Her skin warmed even in the snow. She murmured, "Not until two years ago."

"What?"

"New law. You can appeal the parole."

"What?"

She nodded. "Jason Chernow can appeal the parole. Did you check to see if he's still in?"

"I... I mean I didn't... Why would... he *was... no.* He is in prison! He's in Seattle!"

Ella pulled out her phone, her fingers shaking. She was forced to open the door to the car to get light and warmth and to protect her screen. She apologized softly to Terry as she ducked in, and began typing, her fingers a flurry. Baker shifted uncomfortably behind her, watching, his feet crunching in the snow.

And Ella continued to type.

She opened the portal to current inmates. And searched. Chernow, Jason.

Entered.

And it opened. She stared. The man was covered in prison tattoos. Sloppy, poorly done work. The idiot had even dyed his eyes black, using a needle. She'd seen it before among prisoners. One man, she'd known, had gone completely blind. She cursed, staring at the phone, reading the incarceration dates, double-checking, and then turning, jutting the phone at Baker. "Released two weeks ago," she said, her voice shaking.

Baker gaped.

"Two weeks ago, Baker!" she snapped, and then she turned, marching now, moving back up the mountain.

Baker stared after her. "I—I didn't know!"

She looked over her shoulder. "Let me guess... Carrie's trust fund?" she called, making no effort to quiet her voice as she continued to trudge back up the slopes. "A campaign donation? What was it, Baker? What made you lie to your town?"

"I was trying to help an old friend!" he shouted. "I didn't... I didn't know!"

But Ella just turned away. *You damn fool,* she thought. "Take them somewhere warm and safe. Get Terry a cheeseburger with bacon for me. Extra fries." She was yelling now, marching away, refusing to look back. She'd given her word to Terry. She wouldn't have cared if he'd actually been the murderer—she would've still kept her word. Plus, though she'd never admit it too loudly, part of her felt a strange sense of sympathy for the awkward, odd, gangly teenager. She yelled in finality, "And whatever drink he wants!"

The snow stung, her legs hurt. Her feet were numb.

Her body wanted to quit, but this was the best part. Her anger, the suppressed frustration, she could feel it as fuel. Could feel her controlled temper as nitro. Adrenaline stirring, just waiting to be accessed. Baker was still calling after her, but she didn't reply.

What more could she have expected from someone who'd married into the family?

Family.

They used the word like a cudgel.

Because the Porter family *was* that. A blunt weapon used to beat others into submission. Baker had either taken a kickback, some campaign donation. *Something.* And he'd lied to a town. Or at least, let them believe a lie.

Justifying it because Jason was supposedly in prison.

But not anymore.

Jason Chernow was on this mountain. And he was hunting Maddie Porter. Maddie hadn't been in town when her friend group had chosen to testify.

But Jason had killed his own sister for turning on him. Ella severely doubted he'd show any mercy for Maddie.

She broke into a sprint now.

Not a jog. Not a run.

A dead sprint, racing up the mountain, in the blizzard, breathing heavily, cold air whisking into her lungs. But she didn't look back, didn't slow. Adrenaline now pulsed through her, carrying her faster, faster up the mountain. Back towards where Brenner waited at base camp.

Armed with information.

Maddie was still in danger.

The *real* Mockingbird was still out there.

CHAPTER 16

Brenner drove the snowmobile, and Ella held tightly onto his shoulders this time. She didn't want to lose contact—if she slipped off the back, she wanted him to know it.

They were going slower than she would've liked, but the conditions made it impossible to go fast.

They sped up the slope, cutting through freshly fallen snow—the worst conditions for snowmobiling. Brenner shouted, "Told you—we're gonna get stuck!"

"Go until we do!" she yelled.

He shook his head, stood to his feet, still gripping the handlebars, and leaned forward as if willing the machine forward.

"He was in the tree, Brenner!" she yelled over the sounds of the engine and the wind.

"What?"

"The damn tree—I saw where he jumped from. He was in the tree after chumming the camp."

"Like chum, chum?"

"Bear bait," she said. "I checked the bag. Some sort of combination of pheromones and bait. Patent-pending," she said sarcastically. "Zeke made it. Jason got it from his dad."

"Shit... So Jason really is alive?"

"Can we go faster?"

"No."

Ella's fingers tightened against her partner's shoulders. The blizzard was in full effect now. She couldn't see too far in front. Even the headlights, shining brightly from the snowmobile, barely illuminated their path through the angry flurries.

Jason wasn't the only killer on the mountain.

The snow was out here too.

Plus... white fur. James had said.

White fur. Bear bait. Zeke's job had to do with wildlife and animal control—that's what her search had said back in the SUV, when pairing down potential suspects. But white fur. A big, ten foot monster.

Jason had been hiding in the tree, which explained the marks she'd seen. Him and his stupid tattooed eyes.

White fur... white...

"Brenner... I think Jason has a polar bear."

"What?"

"I think he has a *polar bear.* Now *please,*" she said, tight-lipped, "can we go any faster?"

"Still to the commune, you're sure?"

"It's the only place we haven't checked yet. Yes... Please. Faster."

"Alright... if we go flying off a cliff though, I'm telling St. Peter it was your fault."

"Faster."

He didn't reply, the engine roaring, and he continued to lean forward, adding weight to the front of the machine as they labored through the thick snow, hastening along the trails marked by the occasional orange flag.

No sign of Priscilla or her officers. No sign of a soul on this desolate mountainside.

They sped recklessly through the night.

***

Maddie shivered, leaning back and touching at her wounded flank, feeling tears in her eyes from the pain. She hated crying. She'd done too much of it over the last few years.

Ever since her dad had gotten sick.

But those nails had done a number on her ribs. Her fingers came away stained in blood. And now the howl of the blizzard only grew louder.

She hadn't dared to move for... how long? Ten minutes? Ten hours?

She didn't know. It was dark, she had no watch, her phone was out of battery, and she was bleeding in a stall full of muck.

Worst of all, though, was the giant, two-ton lump wheezing where it lay in the center of the barn, blocking any access whatsoever to the exit. Now that she'd gotten a better look at it, she felt silly.

It wasn't some fairy-tale monster.

It was worse.

A *real* monster, with white fur and a big, black nose, and teeth big enough to rip her head off. The white fur was in clumps, though, suggesting the bear had been shaved. And when polar bears were shaved, it gave them a downright demonic appearance. Black skin with slabs of muscle and sinew, muzzles like some werewolf, skeletal and pronounced. Parts of the bear's fur had been left, but matted and jutting and wild like clumps of grass. It didn't look much like a bear... and perhaps that had been the point.

She hadn't known Nome had *polar* bears... What the hell was a polar bear doing here? Didn't they belong in the North Pole? No... wait. South Pole? Was Nome *in* the North Pole?

She wished she'd paid closer attention in Geography.

But now she just leaned back against the thick plank wall, portions reinforced by nails and wooden beams. The reinforcements, clearly, were for the big old beast now slumbering on top of a crinkling packet of something which smelled like death.

She couldn't stay here, though. She'd die... Either of cold, starvation, dehydration or... bear attack.

She shivered. If the man with the demonic eyes returned, it would be just as bad as that last option. No pupils—black eyeballs. She'd never seen it before and she never wanted to see it again.

The bear growled, pawing at its face. It didn't look particularly hungry. And the red streaks around its muzzle only aroused horrible imaginings.

Maddie bit her lip, if only to introduce her body to the concept of pain. And then she slowly inched up the wall, moving over the boards, trying not to snag on anything jutting. As she did, her ribs throbbed, and she muffled a sob.

The bear shifted.

She froze.

The bear growled, teeth showing, but then it settled again, still laying on its side. It hadn't smelled her. Or perhaps it was still too full from its last meal to bother. She glanced up. The hole she'd come through was far too high.

She couldn't reach it.

She glanced across towards the water barrel that the black-eyed man had rolled in front of the wooden boards, blocking the one spot where she'd seen a gap. Broken, splintered wood. And an opening.

Wide enough for her to crawl through?

She hoped so. Her side was already on fire. She wondered if the rust from the nails had already killed her. Maybe she just didn't know it yet.

But also, her jacket was shredded along the side. Heat was escaping. It was only a matter of time. She couldn't stay here.

The commune was three miles... *that* way?

No... no, that way. Wait... She scowled, trying to remember which direction she'd been heading. Away from the front doors. Yes... that was right. She nodded to herself. East? No... West... Wait.

She scowled. Who the hell cared? Geography wasn't her strong suit. Or directions. Or damn polar bears.

She shook her head, moving around the stall, shivering as she did but trying to keep as quiet as possible. She slipped along the top of the stall, pausing as the wood creaked. She winced, licking her lips and glancing towards the barn door.

The black-eyed man was gone. He must've left. She didn't know where to... but he was gone. For now. She had to hurry.

But the bear was directly between her and the water barrel.

She winced, glancing towards the front door. What about there? N o... no, she'd heard the bar slide into place.

Her best bet was the thin opening behind the barrel. She shivered a bit and closed her eyes, summoning inner strength. Just like her aunt Priscilla. She'd never seen someone as stubborn as Cilla Porter.

She smiled at the thought of her aunt. And then she moved, slipping down the stall, into the main barn area.

The bear's eyes were closed. It breathed heavily, laying there. She spotted faint scars along the thing's back and ears. Someone clearly hadn't been very kind to the creature.

She felt her heart well with sympathy, but just as quickly, she admonished the emotion, suppressing it.

This was *not* something Aunt Priscilla was very good at. Keeping her emotions to herself. Maddie hadn't seen someone yell so much since her father during the last Superbowl.

Still... Aunt Priscilla was tough as nails...

Maddie winced. Tough as... something other than nails.

She used this memory, this borrowed courage, to sneak around the bear. Tiptoeing quietly, trying to give it a wide berth.

Something crinkled.

She froze, directly behind the bear's great rump.

The creature lifted its head slowly, sniffing at the air. She glanced sharply down, realizing she'd stepped on the bag the killer had tossed into the barn.

She couldn't quite make out the text on the front of the silver container, but the lettering created a sort of circle.

She glanced at the bear, exhaled slowly and waited, willing it to go back to sleep.

The polar bear shifted its great bulk, grumbled a bit more like a cantankerous old man, then settled again, resting its head on its paws.

It really was quite cute. Or would've been if not for its teeth.

Those scars she'd spotted laced all the way down its back, as if someone had whipped the poor thing.

A poor thing that ate your friends, probably, she thought to herself.

She took another step away from the crinkling package, moving slowly, cautiously, breathing plumes of steam.

The blizzard outside the barn was hardly welcoming. But it whined and groaned and rose in volume. The bear didn't seem cold, and she resisted the urge to find something to cover it with.

A strange thing the mind. Compassion for a killer animal...

But it wasn't a monster. Just a bear.

Which meant the man with the black eyes...

Just a man.

She reached the water barrel. Just a man. He was just a man, she reminded herself. He wouldn't find her. He couldn't. She'd get to the commune, would escape the snow.

She pushed the water barrel, trying to make as little noise as possible. Just a man.

Just a man sitting above her, staring down at her through the slats in the boards with those black eyes.

"I knew you were here," he said in a singsong voice.

She couldn't help herself. She screamed and shoved the barrel with all her might. The polar bear roared, disturbed from its slumber. And, wedging between the barrel and the wall, she hurtled through the gap in the boards. A *thump*. The man had landed behind her, laughing.

The polar bear was snarling, growling, beginning to move.

"Stay back, big boy, or you get the whip!" yelled the man's voice.

Maddie clambered through the hole, her jacket sleeves in the snow, pulling herself forward. She was still screaming. How strange. She noticed it like a distant observer.

She crawled along the powder, her legs still behind. She pushed through the opening. Her second leg followed. She tried to gasp, but then a hand shot out, snaring her foot, pulling *hard*.

She screamed.

"Come back here! Come on!" yelled Jasmine's voice excitedly.

Maddie screamed some more and kicked. Kicked harder. Her foot caught a wrist. A yell of pain. He squeezed, her ankle protesting in pain. But she slipped free.

Her boot came off. But she managed to pull away. Desperate now, scrambling in the snow, her foot instantly soaked and frozen, she stumbled away. She broke into a sprint, without looking back.

Running again. She didn't even notice which way she was going. She just needed to run. Faster... to run faster.

Her toes were throbbing from the cold. Numb suddenly.

Frostbite would set in within moments.

The rusted nails along her side could cause lockjaw. Worse...

Maddie wasn't sure if she would ever see her father again. But the thought of the possibility propelled her desperately forward, scrambling into the trees while a voice, almost a combination of Jasmine and Carrie, screamed after her.

CHAPTER 17

The snowmobile had stopped. No matter how much Brenner tried, they couldn't get it going again. Ella had already abandoned the thing and was marching through the snow. It was now up to her knees, and the blizzard was only intensifying.

Brenner yelled, "We have to go back, Ella!"

She didn't even reply, continuing forward.

"Dammit, Ella! You're going to get us killed!"

Ella kept going, doggedly moving forward. No sign of Priscilla. No sign of the other cops. She wondered if they'd already reached the commune.

Brenner cursed, then turned the headlights to light their path as best he could, leaving the snowmobile running. It would be no good on their way back except, perhaps—the heat of the engine melting the falling snow—as a guiding light, like a lighthouse.

And then he began to trudge after her.

She shot him a quick look and breathed slowly. "You can go back!" she yelled. "She's my cousin!"

"You don't have to do this just because Cilla is! Your sister has a team of cops. A bunch of provisions, first aid—I even saw some battery heaters."

"I'm not doing this for Cilla!" Ella yelled.

Brenner just growled and fell into step.

"I said go back!"

"Shut up" he snapped, trudging ahead of her in answer, and beginning to do his best to push down the snow to clear the way.

"What's that ahead?" Ella said suddenly.

Brenner followed her finger. He yelled. "Cilla. That's them—is that a barn?"

"I think so. Means the commune is only a few miles ahead. Come on... We're almost there."

Brenner nodded, still trudging through the snow, pushing it out of the way, and breathing heavily as he did.

Ella had already spent her adrenaline and now she was moving forward on pure, undistilled will. One foot after the other. One step after the next.

She didn't stop. And neither did the marshal.

***

Ella stumbled forward, gasping, and catching herself on the nearest cop, grabbing her arm.

Except it wasn't a cop. "Get off me!" snapped Cilla.

Her twin sister whirled, glaring at Ella, but then stopped, staring. Ella's face felt like a million needles were being slowly probed against it. She was breathing so heavily she couldn't catch her breath or even speak. She held up a single finger, asking for a second to gather herself, ever polite.

Cilla, for perhaps the first time in her existence, didn't have a word to say. She stood amidst the cops she'd taken up the mountain, all of them heating by a small fire built into a rusted water barrel. She watched as Ella gathered her breath, a look of... *respect* lingering there.

And then she spotted Brenner trudging behind, and her expression morphed to disdain.

"Well, aren't you too cute? Suicide pact, is it?"

Neither of them responded, both still catching their breaths. Ella gave a quick count of the cops with Cilla. Nine of them. Thompson, the tenth, had left. All accounted for. At least there was that.

When she'd finally regained her breath, Ella said, "It's Jason Chernow."

Cilla had been giving instructions to one of her officers—though, they were more like her *husband's* officers, but Ella got the distinct impression that the police department didn't see much of a difference between the authority of Chief Baker and his wife.

Besides, if she had to guess, Baker had gotten his position from donations in the Porter family's name. Same as he'd likely gotten from Jason Chernow or Carrie Chernow's trust fund. Hush money.

And now three teens were dead.

Ella straightened, having regained her breath, looking her sister directly in the eyes. "It's Jason," she said again.

Cilla frowned. "He's in..." She caught herself. "He's dead."

Ella stared. "So you did know?"

"Is that accusation in your tone, sister? What now? Did I strangle your puppy? Sleep with your boyfriend?" She smirked—somehow finding the energy for pettiness despite their predicament.

Ella hesitated, shooting a look at Brenner. She'd seen a kiss, but not...

No, no, not important. "Jason Chernow was paroled two weeks ago," she said. "I think his dad had a pet bear."

"A what? A bear?"

"Yeah. He works with wildlife capture. It's called *Fauna Solutions*—I saw polar bears on their website. I think he probably took a bear and kept it or something. Maybe trained it. He's got this miracle bear tonic."

"Are you okay? Are you feverish?"

"No... it's like this bait. Anyway," Ella said, shaking her head. "Have we checked the barn?"

"Yeah. Nothing. No one. But... speaking of miracle tonic." Cilla reached into her pocket. There was a crinkling sound and she pulled out a small, familiar, silver pouch. On the front, in circular lettering, it read *Zeke's Miracle Bear Bait.*

She shoved it towards Ella's face and only then said, "Careful, it reeks."

Ella didn't need the admonishment. She was already jerking her head back, wincing and wrinkling her nose. "That's potent," she muttered, remembering Terry's comment about James being woken by a smell.

She carefully avoided pushing her sister's hand away, as the last thing she wanted was to offend Cilla while surrounded by men with guns who answered to her.

The cops had moved through the barn, but one of them was pointing at the front door. "This is troubling," the man was saying.

Brenner approached, and Ella watched. Brenner grunted, then lifted a long splinter nearly the length of his arm. He kicked a thick plank of wood, which had been lodged to keep the door shut. "Something broke through here," he said. He nodded at the pack in Cilla's hand. "Guessing it wasn't anything small."

"Hey! I found something!"

Another voice. This time from where a cop was peering along the side of the barn. He waved them over. Ella stepped forward, Cilla shoved past her, and Ella allowed her sister the lead. Priscilla paused, staring. "Those are footsteps!" she said suddenly, pointing at impressions in the ground.

"Two sets!" Brenner yelled. "They lead to the commune."

Ella spotted a gap in the side of the barn, just big enough for a person to fit through. The footsteps in the snow were nearly filled, though, little more than faint dimples against the white. They were lucky they'd spotted them when they had. Any longer, and it was likely they might have been completely buried under the snow.

Ella found her heart thumping now. Two figures in the snow. Only one camper remaining. And one killer at large.

Maddie Porter and the murderer, who she was confident was Jason Chernow.

Nothing else made sense.

The cops were all glancing at the sisters. Brenner was also watching, motionless, waiting. And then, neither glancing at the other, the twins seemed to reach a decision simultaneously.

Both of them stepped into the snow. The barn had been providing some small amount of cover, but both of them disdained this in favor of forward motion.

One step at a time, they both trudged through the snow, side by side, neither glancing at the other, both marching forward. The figures behind them grimly fell into step. Brenner and the cops seemed to have decided it was best not to argue with the Porter sisters when they got in such a mood.

Ella was back on adrenaline but running on fumes. Still, her features were a mask, even under the snow, refusing to allow a crack in the facade.

Priscilla, on the other hand, was cursing and muttering every step, shaking her head and fist at the ground as if somehow she wanted to punch and kick every snowflake in sight.

They moved along the snow, marching forward. But it was slow going, and the terrain was treacherous. Ella had no clue where the trail was now... nor if there were any drop-offs on either side.

Ella moved quickly alongside her sister, breathing heavily as she did.

Every now and then, one of the cops would toss a flare, both ahead of them, and behind them, marking their way, but also leaving a trail for them to follow. Sparking, red light pulsed from the snow. Glow sticks were also employed, attached to trees, or on rocks. But snow often buried these, swallowing the breadcrumb trail home.

But onward they moved.

"See that ahead?" someone was saying.

Ella just about glimpsed the lights shining from a mountain-side town. The commune, she guessed. Off-gridders gathered together. According to Thompson, one of the leaders had been making eyes at his sister.

Ella had considered the possibility of his involvement in all of this, but the MO didn't match. No—she felt Jason Chernow was their suspect. The commune was a distraction.

At least... so she hoped.

But then again, the footprints in the snow seemed to be leading directly towards the place. After about ten minutes, they lost sign of any tracks, the snow completely burying them.

One of the cops suddenly yelled, and another snatched his arm, yanking him back from where he'd nearly tumbled off a cliff.

"This is moronic!" the cop screamed. "Ms. Porter, we need to head back!"

"Go on then!" Ella and Cilla both shouted. They both shot each other a suspicious look and kept going.

Ella felt a pang of guilt again. Another horrible choice. Did she really want to lead anyone off the edge of a cliff? She shivered, remembering an experience in Thailand, on vacation with one of her old partners. The two had gone cave-diving during flood season. They'd nearly drowned, trapped in water for nearly a day as they moved through tight, claustrophobic tunnels.

The whole experience had been exhilarating, but only afterwards had Ella wondered if she'd been the reason her partner had followed her into the tunnels.

She didn't want to be the cause of anyone's death.

And so she turned, waving an arm. "Head back! Brenner, you can lead them!"

Cilla looked over but didn't say a word. "Babies," she muttered. She continued forward. Ahead, a large, jutting rock formation extended over the trail, suggesting it was blocking their current path... unless of course the trail wrapped around the rock, but this was a guess at best, as the snow was so thick, clinging to every surface, that it was difficult to tell where stone lay beneath or simply open air.

Brenner had ignored her call, though, and kept up with the two sisters.

A few of the other cops were veering off, however. Five, in fact, were now moving back, following the flares and glowsticks and orange flags.

Four others held a quiet, grim conference, but then pressed on, following.

"Ten ounces each," Cilla called to each of them. "And if anyone dies, the others get his share!"

This seemed to revive some of the lack of energy visible in the cops. Ten ounces of pure gold was as much as sixteen thousand dollars after clean-up and processing. It took months for Ella to match that. But to her sister, it was as easy as waving a wand.

Brenner was now marching side by side with Ella, clearly favoring his left leg, occasionally massaging his limping right without complaint.

And it was as they rounded the stone protrusion, finding solid footing in the ground, that Ella and Brenner went still.

"Hear that?" Brenner said suddenly.

She did. Cilla was still growling and cursing, though.

Ella caught her sister's arm. Cilla ripped her wrist free, but the silence they'd gained caused her to go still and listen as well.

Now all of them stared around the side of the stony protrusion. A deep, low growl was emanating from the snow.

Ella slowly reached for her firearm.

Brenner's leapt into his hand in the blink of an eye, like an extension of him. Ella had never seen someone as fast on the draw as the ex-sniper.

Cilla was now gesturing at the other cops to come around them. They were all shivering, motionless. The growling intensified. But Ella couldn't see a thing. Even with the flashlights, perched on the narrow ledge of stone, amidst ice and wind, snowflakes pouring down with wild abandon, she couldn't see.

The growling intensified. A throaty warning. They were encroaching on some unseen beast's territory, and if they didn't back off, the thing would make them.

But Ella didn't know *where* to retreat to. She tried to step back, bumped into a cop. The man cursed. She felt his gun brush against her arm. She caught herself. The man fired in the dark, whether by accident or because he'd seen something, she didn't know.

But two flashes from a muzzle. Loud *cracks*. The snow illuminated as if touched by lightning as the gun fired.

The growl turned into a roar. A thunder of paws against the snow. And a polar bear came surging around the stone barrier, kicking through the snow.

Ella only spotted it because of an errant flashlight beam. Other beams were off over the cliff or back along the trail, all attempting to locate the source of the noise. Ella heard another scream. More gunshots. More lights caught it, illuminating it more clearly. Ella's heart leapt. The creature didn't quite *look* like a bear. It's skin was black, for one, and covered in scars. Clumps of white fur jutted like tufts of weeds from the black skin. The face was gaunt and skeletal, lips the same color as coal pulled back in a snarl to reveal sharp thumb-sized teeth.

The bear wasn't trying to hurt them but run—it seemed—*past* them. The fear in its eyes was evident. But as it came towards them, its attention shifted. It snapped out at one of the cops, ripping the jacket. A howl of pain.

And then gunfire erupted. More roaring. Ella was knocked flying. Her heart in her throat. She tumbled back. The cop who'd fallen into her grabbed her arm and fell as well.

The chill of open air embraced her as Ella's feet stumbled for ground that no longer existed. And the last thing she glimpsed, stumbling over the cliff, was the sight of Brenner.

His eyes flashed—a split-second of instinct, and then he holstered his gun and dove over the cliff after her. It was only in that split-second, when his foot had been on solid ground crossing into open air, that his eyes widened, as if realizing what he'd done. A momentary, split-second glimpse of alarm.

And then the three of them, Ella, Brenner and the cop, tumbled off the side of the cliff.

CHAPTER 18

SHE HIT THE ICE and went straight through with a sound between a crack and a splash, as if going through a windshield. And she was instantly inundated in freezing, cold water.

She thrashed about, desperate, tried to rise, but her head bumped against a layer of ice. She kicked, redirecting, tried to rise again, another bump against the ice. This time it had some give. Bubbles escaped her lips. She kicked about. The freezing water lashed at her, nipped at her skin, biting deep.

Ella shivered horribly, desperate, shoving her hands up against a literal, glass ceiling. She continued to push. She felt a tug at her leg but couldn't see a thing in the murk. Her fingers found an opening in the ice—the same place she'd come through. With desperation, freezing, she pulled herself up, fingers slipping on the ice.

She managed to surge through. The hand grasping at her leg, used her as a guide. She scrambled—gasping and breathing heavily, soaked to the bone—onto the thin layer of the ice. Snow fell about her, and it only worsened the shivering.

But she turned, slipping along on her chest, moving on the ice and reaching back. The hand on her leg had held firm. She managed to pull the cop up behind her.

"Are you okay?" she tried to scream. But it came out as mostly chattering and faint moaning. Her own body was rejecting her attempts to speak.

The man was also frozen, shaking horribly. He stumbled and she did too. But their coats were no longer serving any purpose except to hold them down, laden with ice-cold water. She wasn't sure what was worse, the elements or the ice.

Hypothermia was the main threat. They could be dead in minutes.

She took a step, tugging the cop along. But her foot fell through the ice with a horrible *crack!* She yelled, but this time he caught her.

She glanced up and could no longer hear the gunshots or the snarling. How far had they fallen?

She spotted a sudden light. Twenty feet to her left. She moved towards it, trying to call out, but it was as if her throat had seized up.

Shock, she realized. Her body was going into shock. Even stepping forward seemed a difficult thing.

She moved as quickly as she could, stumbling on the ice. Another crack, but this time her foot didn't go through.

Brenner was yelling now. He was covered in snow, and behind him, wedged against the cliff an *enormous* bank of gathered, old snow and sludge. This, she guessed, was what he'd hit. At least he wasn't soaked in freezing water.

Brenner caught one look at the sight of the two of them and started waving his arm like a windmill.

He'd jumped off a cliff after her. Insane. Absolutely insane. It was as if he hadn't realized what he'd been doing. Brenner had always been that way, hadn't he? Throwing himself between his father's fist and his mother. Putting himself in harm's way for another.

He'd done it again, and she wished she wasn't so absolutely frozen stiff and could appreciate it more.

Brenner, though, knew they were on a ticking clock. He pulled both of them off the small, mountain lake. The cracks in the ice being hastily covered by the stucco of snow. "Here!" he yelled. "There—the rocks! Use the shelf!"

He was pointing ahead, guiding them along the side of the cliff, under a shelf of stone.

The stone served to give a very small amount of shelter, and Ella thought that the shelf itself looked ready to collapse at any moment. But the possibility of being buried alive was secondary to the certainty of freezing to death.

"A damn polar bear," Brenner was saying, his voice trembling. "My God. Alright... here—here! Anything paper. Anything... Wood? No—shit, no wood. So what..." Brenner was hastily patting at his pockets. He paused, then ripped out his wallet, moving hastily. A few dollar bills and a fiver were tossed on the ground. Then a gym membership card made of cheap cardboard. He also ripped out some of the fabric lining. And last, he hesitated. A folded piece of paper, secured in a safe spot behind a plastic strip... A letter, by the look of it... Or no... no crayon. A child's drawing?

Brenner stared at the thing for a moment, and he let out a faint wheezing sound as if in some form of physical pain, but then he cursed and tossed the paper next to the bills. Wind tried to scatter the items, but he stamped on it with his foot.

Ella pulled out the bear bait she'd found in Zeke's pocket. "Might still be dry!" she said, shivering. "The outside looks waterproof."

Again, her words barely came, more like a whisper between bursts of chattering.

Brenner took it from her, ripped it open, and dumped the noxious-smelling content on the ground. Like pieces of beef jerky, or shredded wool. The stench arose and even the wind couldn't carry it away.

"Not enough... God damn—you two, stay here. You—hey, hey, listen. Light this! Now!" Brenner shoved a spare flare into the hand of the cop. The man, dripping horribly, approached, trembling, and then Brenner pushed away from the cliff, sprinting into the snow.

Ella tried to call after him, but the words again died on her tongue.

She watched as the cop bent and tried to start the flare, but his hands were trembling so badly, he failed twice. Ella bent too, taking it from him, and she managed to light it. She then pressed the sparking end against the meager kindling Brenner had supplied. The crayon drawing went up first.

The money next. And the lint-like lining smoked more than burnt.

She watched the kindling catch fire, burning. Then the small portions of bait, shaped like jerky, caught fire—beginning to smoke but then sputter flames.

Her heart leapt in hope. She tried to lean back to avoid dripping.

She ripped off her jacket, tossing it on the ground, shivering so violently, she nearly collapsed. But the coat was of no help now, soaked as it was, it was only threatening the burgeoning flames—and even without it, occasional droplets of water tapped against the flames, hissing and sizzling out of existence.

"Got it!" Brenner's voice screeched in delight. He hastened back in a sprint, stumbling on his right leg, and hitting the wall. But he was already ripping at something in his hand. A dead branch. Soaked by snow evidently, but he was cutting at it with a knife, peeling back as much of the damp bark as possible.

He didn't peel it off but instead, made it into feathers, cutting slowly. And then he tossed this strange, whittled, feathered piece of wood onto the small fire. He turned and sprinted away again.

A few moments later, he returned with more sticks. And some moss. The moss just smoked. "Too wet," he spat. He tossed these away.

Then the sticks. Building a small sort of tepee.

"Strip!" Brenner yelled now. "Both of you—now!"

The cop was already undressing. Ella was too freezing cold to blush. She began to undress hurriedly as well. As she did, her socks, her boots, her pants, and her secondhand sweater joining her secondhand coat, the fire began to rise.

Ella hadn't ever before realized how *painful* cold could be. It almost felt worse than a burn, as if every nerve ending in her body was screaming at once. And there was nothing she could do about it.

As she removed her top, Brenner pulled his jacket off, holding it near her to help conceal her modesty.

The cop didn't care. He was down to his underwear and was now crouched by the growing fire, blowing on the flames with shuddering breaths.

Ella gave Brenner a quick nod of gratitude as he wrapped his jacket around her shoulders. Now he was shivering as well.

The three of them stood in the smoke, which spilled up the side of the overhanging shelf of rock, caught under the outcrop before dispersing to the night, lifting on the wind in curls of gray.

The fire continued to grow, and now, crouched, using Brenner's coat for both warmth and modesty, Ella drew as near as she could. The cop was trembling as well, next to her. Brenner pulled off his long-sleeved shirt, tossing it to the man, who accepted it gratefully, pulling it on.

Now—Brenner in his t-shirt, the other two still wet, down to their underwear and freezing—they gathered near the blaze, indifferent if they inhaled smoke or not, just letting the rising flames warm them.

After about a minute, the fire began to eat at the wood completely. Brenner pumped his fist, though his teeth were chattering. He held up a finger as if to say *one moment,* turned and sprinted off again.

Ella didn't even have the strength to call out this time.

He returned once more, this time with a large branch, as long as he was tall, dragging it through the snow. At a bit over six foot, Brenner had to duck to re-enter their hidden alcove—he also had to snap a portion of this branch for it to enter as well. He tossed pieces on the fire. His hands moving in a blur.

Now, Ella—her gloves discarded—extended her fingers to the fire. She sat there huddled against the wall as the fire kept growing.

Brenner slowly lowered himself as well. A pile of spare wood chunks near his right hand. The cop across from them was no longer trembling violently. His back was to the snow, but Brenner's long-sleeved shirt was protecting him from the worst of the blizzard's assault.

Brenner looked about a moment and then retreated once more. She watched as he began scooping snow, using it to create a small wind barrier. He used his foot, his hands, shoving the snow fast until it mounted up quickly. Like this, he blocked off four feet of space between the ground and the ceiling of the rock shelf.

Now, the wind blew above them, meeting the smoke, but the snow didn't enter the space as much. The combination of this new snow wall and the cliff face with the outcrop gave them three sides of shelter.

Brenner slipped around the side of his makeshift wall.

"Gotta leave some space for the smoke," he said, teeth chattering. His hands were trembling now. Ella shot him a quick look, snatched at his hand, her own fingers still shaking, and tugged him insistently towards the fire.

As she did, the front of the jacket slipped. She caught Brenner's brief stare, then he looked away, seeming suddenly embarrassed.

The proportion she was growing warm was the same level to which her own embarrassment grew. It was still only a flicker of an ember, but she could feel it being fanned.

The cop was too dog-tired and cold to care one lick about the female form, but Brenner and she had history. And clearly things weren't exactly settled between them.

Now, Ella secured his jacket tighter around her, but she still held on to his arm, guiding him back to a spot by the fire. He lowered slowly, refusing now to look at her at all, as if for penance for glancing at her breasts.

Ella closed her eyes, inhaling slowly, and after a bit, leaned back to avoid inhaling smoke, using the wall as something of a support.

Brenner also leaned against the wall. The cop remained with his back to the snow.

"W-what's your name?" Ella said, glancing at the man.

He looked over, wincing. He had fair hair, like Brenner's, but a wider face. His eyes had crinkles in the corners—laugh lines. Such lines were nowhere present on Brenner's countenance.

"Malcolm," he said softly.

"N-nice t-t-to meet you, M-Malcolm," she said.

He nodded wearily and turned his attention back to the life-giving fire. Brenner, now that everyone was warming, leaned back, breathing in, out, slowly trying to calm his nerves.

A few moments later and Ella was no longer shivering. The fire warmed her, and she'd never been so grateful for the stench of Zeke's miracle bait before.

The smoke assaulted her nostrils, but she didn't care. Brenner wearily reached out, scraping some more snow to allow the smoke more space to escape, but then he collapsed back against the wall like a suddenly dropped anchor.

His arms went limp against his sides.

The three of them remained there for a few minutes, and then Ella began to move. Dignity be damned, even though she could feel Brenner watching her every time she turned about and fetched an article of clothing, she had to hurry.

"What are you doing?" Malcolm asked.

"You should too," she warned. "We need to dry our clothes. Quickly."

Malcolm hesitated. "R-right... I mean—they'll find us, yeah?"

"Probably. Eventually." Ella tossed her coat onto the rock between Brenner and her, near the fire. "But," Ella said, "Madison is still out there."

"You're joking," Malcolm murmured. "Really? Still? It's over. There was a goddamn polar bear up there!" he said, his voice a moan. "We fell off a cliff. We nearly drowned. We nearly froze. Just... it's over."

She shrugged. *Maybe for you, it is,* she thought. But out loud, she simply said. "That's fine. Just rest." She kept planting articles of clothing out. She then drew nearer to the fire again, allowing her undergarments, which she still wore, to dry as well.

The wet mark on the cold stone beneath her was slowly evaporating as well.

Brenner just stared at her, incredulous. "You really are something," he said.

"Maddie doesn't have fire," Ella replied quietly. "How long for this all to dry?"

Brenner shrugged. "Could take hours."

"Any way to speed it up?"

A sigh. "I can think of a few. More fire—wringing them out, then stretching them out on a sort of Y-branch. Yeah. Maybe an hour, then. Could still be damp. That'll kill you."

"An hour... Fine... if that..." Ella bit her lip. If Maddie was out in this for another hour, she was undoubtedly dead. Hell, for all Ella knew, Maddie was already dead. She hadn't seen her cousin in twelve years.

According to Priscilla, Maddie and Ella were somewhat similar. Not that Ella really knew what this meant. But still... an hour... or dead. Then no one could help Maddie.

"Think Priscilla was eaten by that bear?" Brenner murmured.

Ella shot him a look. "You almost sound hopeful."

"What? Oh... no... no," he said, tired. "I guess not."

Ella watched him. The cop was arranging his own clothing by the fire now, but also bunching it up, using it as bedding. He rested his head against it. Ella glanced down at her own toes. Nothing blue. She moved them. She could feel them.

That was a small miracle. Her fingers too. She checked her ears... No frostbite. A definite miracle. Just like Zeke's product advertised.

A few more minutes of silence, warmth, and Brenner occasionally replacing the wood on the fire gave way to the cop's snoring. Brenner returned a bit later with more wood, and also a couple of branches shaped like a Y.

"Too wet to burn," he said, "but fine for this."

He propped her jacket on one. Her shirt on the other. Then set up a crossbeam between them and dangled her pants along these.

Now, Ella stared at her pants attached to the wooden pole and blushed. She hunched lower, arms wrapped around her knees, grateful for Brenner's jacket.

This time, he had the modesty not to glance at her.

The snoring from the cop intensified, his face, though, even in slumber, carrying a look of fear. Ella was tapping her foot against the stone. In part, simply grateful she still had all her toes.

But also, in part, out of impatience and a desire to count down the seconds. An hour was too long.

"Half an hour," Ella said suddenly.

Brenner grunted.

"I mean it. We can't stay here."

"No, but the blizzard will pass by morning."

"We can't stay. We'll get snowed in."

"Ella, I can't make water dry faster."

"Half an hour. Look, it's almost dry already!" She squeezed her pants. Definitely damp. She scowled, slumping back, defeated.

"Just rest," he said. "You can't do everything." He shot her a sidelong glance, then settled as well.

"Brenner..." Ella said in a small voice.

"Mhmm?"

More snoring from the cop. Brenner's eyes were drooping now too. He tossed another piece of wood on the fire then pinched himself on the arm, forcing his eyes open again. "Don't let me drift off," he muttered. "We have to keep this stoked."

"Do you think she's still alive?"

"Maddie or Priscilla?"

"Either."

"I don't know."

Ella sighed again, staring at the flames. She glanced over where the bright glow caught the blue of Brenner Gunn's gaze. She stared at him for a second, her eyes moving towards his lips. She'd seen him kiss Priscilla with those lips.

She'd never had the courage to ask him before.

That's what it was, wasn't it?

Courage.

At least, that's how Brenner saw it. He thought her politeness, holding back her emotions was all a lie. He didn't think manners were worth much...

And sometimes, she thought this was silly.

But sometimes...

She hated that he had a point.

She didn't *mean* to lie. She didn't think of herself as a coward. But... but why hadn't she ever asked him? Sitting there, warming by the fire, half-naked, exposed and vulnerable, and absolutely exhausted, she found her lips looser than they might have otherwise been.

She murmured. "Why did you do it?"

"Hmm?"

"You..." *Why did you break up with me?* But she chickened out again. Besides, it was more than a decade ago. It was old news. Just silly, childish things. Instead, she said, "You jumped off a cliff."

He blinked, then chuckled. "Yeah. Numbskull move."

"Why?"

"Pure instinct. I didn't even see who had fallen. Just wanted to help, I guess."

She wasn't sure why, but for some reason, this stung. She frowned but hid the expression. In a way, she knew she had *wanted* Brenner to have jumped for her. Not just instinct. Not some training.

"Never lost a man on a mission, you know," Brenner said quietly. "Not when I was on overwatch. Not once. Not in five years." He spoke in such a way that the sadness wasn't as present as usual in his voice. He even smiled.

She liked it when he smiled. He rarely did that. Even back then.

"What was that drawing?"

"Hmm?"

"The one in your wallet."

He stared at the fire now, swallowed. His voice was strained. "Nothing," he said. "Just... yeah... nothing."

She closed her eyes now, calming, warm. She watched as her clothing dried. Brenner shot her a sidelong glance. "You know, if you're warm enough, I don't mind taking my jacket back."

She stared at him. "Umm... are you sure?"

He gave her a sly smirk, then shook his head. "Nah. I'm teasing. Mostly."

"You're an asshole."

"I try, Ella."

"Thanks for saving m—us..." She'd been about to say *me*. But it felt too vulnerable. *Us* felt better. Plausible deniability in a crowd.

Brenner just nodded once. He was staring at the fire again. Those same cut features, that same sad, pretty face. She remembered it all so well.

"You know something, Ella—"

"Why did you break up with me?"

They both went quiet. She inwardly kicked herself. It had just erupted from her lips. She hadn't felt in control of the words.

Brenner scratched at the back of his head. "Er, what?" he said.

He'd heard her. She knew he had, but he was giving her a second chance. An olive branch. An opportunity to take it back, to gloss over it and pretend as if it hadn't been said.

"Why did you break up with me?" she repeated, her voice quiet, gentle, but her eyes fixed on the fire for an excuse not to meet his gaze. She didn't take it back but allowed the question to settle, slow and firm between them.

Chapter 19

"I... just... I mean..."

"You don't... you don't have to tell me. I get it. It's old news. We're all grown-up, aren't we?" She gave a little laugh attempting to be carefree, but it sounded hollow, the dismissiveness buried by her own thumping heart.

"You were too good for me," Brenner said simply. He looked at her now, as if daring her to meet his gaze. He didn't look away. "Ella Porter, Princess of Nome. Just too... *good.*"

She stared at him now. He didn't look away. Neither did she.

"Are you... that... that's a stupid reason, Brenner!" She felt a surge of anger. "A really, really dumb reason. Are you joking?"

"Hey, hang on. I'm baring my heart here."

"And I'm undressed, pretending like you're not trying to catch a peek, but that has to be the most Neanderthal thing I ever heard."

"What is?"

"That *I* was too good for you, so you broke my heart?"

"Your heart? What? I didn't mean to..."

Ella was shaking her head, though, her fingers tight on the jacket. For a moment, she forgot about her clothing over the fire. Forgot about the need for it to dry quickly. Forgot the hiss and sizzle of droplets steaming where they hit the fire.

All she felt was her own flames, rising in her stomach. Her eyes narrowed, her anger rising. For a brief moment, she even felt like Priscilla.

There was so much she wanted to say. So much she wanted to yell at him. Didn't he know? For five years she hadn't had the stomach to date anyone. Her heart had been shattered. She had thought, at the time, they would marry—grow old together. She'd thought he was the one...

Then she'd lost it. She'd lost... everything she'd known. She'd left.

She scowled now. And this only made her feel petulant, which made it worse.

She didn't want to feel like some child throwing a temper-tantrum. People broke up. Mature decisions sometimes ended relationships. But still... what an asinine reason to...

"I'm not," she said. And this was the extent of what she felt capable of voicing out loud. "I'm not at all. I never was. You're... you're as good as anyone I knew, Brenner."

"I didn't mean to kiss your sister."

"Oh-no. No, please. We don't have to. I shouldn't have said anything. It's the smoke."

"I didn't. I thought it was you. I asked Priscilla to get you. I wanted to apologize, to get back together with you. I was drunk." He nodded, his face red, and it wasn't just the glow from the flames. "A damn drunk. Like I said. I was *drunk. Drunk.*" He kept repeating the word as if it were some blade he was gouging into his heart again and again in masochistic repetition.

"What do you mean you thought it was me?"

"Priscilla said you were home," he said glumly. "She said she would go fetch you. She changed clothes. It was dark. I kissed her—but I thought I was kissing you. I realized pretty quick, but I'm guessing you saw us. I was furious. She was laughing."

Ella just stared at Brenner. "You tried to get back together?"

"Ha. Yeah. But... I dunno. You left a couple weeks later. I thought you wanted nothing to do with me. I thought, you know, you were relieved that I'd broken up; finally letting you move on and do what you wanted with your life." Brenner spoke matter-of-factly, transparent in his words, but his emotions, a mask. He'd always been blunt. Able to speak the truth about even the most painful things without hesitation.

She wished, sometimes, she had shared this trait. But now... she wasn't so sure.

"You could have called! Written! Told me!"

"You were gone. You left. What was the point? I was stuck here. I'm still stuck here."

Ella stared at Brenner, frozen in place and seeing him as if in a completely different light. She wasn't sure if this light was better or worse, but it *was* different. And even the soft glow from the flames had nothing to do with it.

She let out a long sigh, tugging at her clothing a bit, seeing if it had dried at all. She shook her head in frustration.

And that's when she heard the scream.

CHAPTER 20

THE SCREAM RESOUNDED THROUGH the night. "Help! Help me!" It carried over the wind and over the blizzard, piercing the barrier of smoke and snow.

Ella was surging to her feet, snatching her clothing and quickly pulling it on.

"It's not dry yet!" Brenner yelled at her.

But the scream resounded again, and Ella nearly lost her cool. "Brenner, let go! It's my cousin."

Brenner stared at her as if stunned. But a final scream seemed to loose his fingers from where he'd snatched at her arm. Her pants were damp, but it would have to do. Her jacket too was damp. She zipped the borrowed jacket fully now, deciding her underclothes had dried as much as they would.

Brenner cursed and jammed something into her hand. His backup gun. She gave a quick nod of gratitude and then turned, pushing through the barrier of snow. Smoke billowed after her.

Another scream. She shot a look back and frowned. Brenner was hastily waking the cop before preparing to follow.

She moved hurriedly around the lake in the direction of the voices, the screaming, but nothing... she spotted nothing, no movement.

Think... dammit. Think.

She hesitated, though it cost her to do so. She froze, shivering and trembling, but focusing on the details, the variables and then...

The cliff.

The voices were echoing off the damn cliff. She was heading in the wrong direction. She spun around and began trudging in the opposite direction, moving quickly. The acoustics along the cliff and ushered by the blizzard played tricks on her, just like the Mockingbird might have wanted.

As she hastened, though, around the lake, peering through the distant forest, she spotted the source of the noise. Movement up ahead. Her heart skipped. Two figures moving through the treeline.

The same treeline Brenner had been getting their firewood from. But the figures hurtled through the branches between the trunks. A smaller figure, a young woman. Running with what looked like a cloth bag wrapped around one foot instead of a boot. She was clutching at her side, rivulets of red streaming down.

And behind her, another figure, racing after the young girl, a glinting knife in one hand.

Ella broke into a sprint, returning once more into the cold. She tried to shout. "Stop! Stop right there!" But her voice was lost in the wind.

Now, the flurries of snow were picking up again. She heard yelling and glanced back to see Brenner charging out as well, wearing her jacket—far too small and damp. He'd borrowed the cop's boots.

She didn't have time to turn him back. Part of her wanted to be frustrated with the man.

But she was beginning to get it.

Something in his DNA.

Something as deep as marrow.

He'd lived his whole life catching blows. In a way, it was almost like he didn't know what to do when he wasn't black and blue.

She didn't slow though, racing forward. She raised her gun, firing as she ran.

The two figures sprinting through the trees both reacted now. The girl, who Ella assumed was Maddie, stumbled, stared, and then screamed, "Help me! He's trying to kill me!"

The man behind her snarled, stopped for a moment, but then lunged. His hand snagged the fleeing girl's hair, pulling *hard*. She stumbled back with a painful cry, and the man dragged her to the ground, screaming in triumph, the knife flashing in his hand. Ella shot, and the man's shoulder jerked back, and he cursed. He managed to hold onto his knife, though.

Now, he ripped Maddie up by her blonde hair, holding her tight, pressing the knife under her throat. Ella approached slowly, weapon in hand—no clean shot. She could hear Brenner breathing heavily as he came up from behind. She kept her gun trained on the killer.

"Jason?" she called out. "Jason Chernow?"

He stared at her. She realized now, his eyes were soot black, both of them stained with prison tattoo ink. He also seemed to hesitate when looking towards her, struggling, it seemed, to track her movement through the woods.

"It's all fine!" Chief Baker's voice barked back. "You can leave now. Thank you, officer!"

It was an uncanny experience. She could detect the flaws in the impression of course. But this was the mimicking murderer. The real Mockingbird, and he did steal voices.

Ella moved through the snow, gun raised. Maddie was sobbing, the knife under her chin. "Cilla!" Maddie was crying. "Please—please, I don't want to die!"

Ella didn't correct her cousin. She kept approaching. The two of them were standing under a large tree with wide branches, temporarily sheltered by the storm. But the snow burdening the branches blocked out any light. Even the flashlight Brenner was pointing now seemed swallowed somewhat by the canopy of darkness.

Ella continued forward, cautious, careful, eyes fixated on the two figures. She inhaled shakily, exhaling a column of steam.

"Get back!" said the man, but in a young woman's voice. "I'm going to hurt her!"

Ella shivered, feeling prickles at the strange voice coming from the man. He had tattoos along his cheeks, his neck. Tattoos all over his body. His eyes gaped at her, dark and without pupils.

Ella took another step forward. She didn't know how to build a fire while soaked, perhaps. And she wasn't known for coordinating search parties.

But this?

Facing a serial killer eye to eye?

This was something as familiar as her own reflection. And in a way, she almost didn't even notice her cousin... A pang of guilt at the realization, but all she could see were those two black eyes. She didn't look away. She didn't blink, not even as snow flurried past her nose. She held a hand up, protecting her face.

"Your father is dead, Jason," she said softly. "And we found the children you murdered.

Maddie was gasping, struggling, knife under her throat. Jason, though, whispered, in Maddie's voice, "Please, Priscilla. Go away!" then in Priscilla's voice, "That's a goddamn order!" He grinned, flashing teeth, not even seeming to notice the blood streaming down his shoulder. As if the combination of adrenaline and snow had numbed him to the pain.

Ella didn't look away. This was a man who cared about his reputation. Had paid off Chief Baker just to save him a public trial. Had copped to the charge for the same reason. This was also a man who was a performer. The voices, the impressions, training animals... This was a man who had wanted to be seen and heard but had never managed to succeed.

She approached one foot after the other, gun gripped tightly.

This man had dyed his eyes for attention. Covered himself with prison tattoos to belong. This was a man who used the voices of *others* to draw the eye and the ear. Had assaulted a woman in his youth because he didn't have the charm or ability to attract one otherwise.

He didn't care that his dad was dead. He'd killed his sister.

A mistake—she realized—to try and jar him by bringing up his father.

So instead, she said, "I like your tattoos."

More fishing. He sneered at her. And then, in his own voice, a very normal voice that wouldn't have caught her attention in any other scenario, he growled, "Get away from here. This is between me and the little tattle tales."

Ella pointed. "Maddie didn't tattle on you. She wasn't even here."

He scowled. "I said get lost! Now! Or I slit her throat. I mean it. I'll do it like I did the others."

Ella nodded slowly. "You were in a tree, right? You chummed the tent, went into the tree, and waited for your bear to attack. A polar bear. Really impressive."

That was the in.

She realized it now.

Not the tattoos. Not the threats.

His damn vanity.

And the vanity was directed towards one performance, wasn't it? It clicked as she realized and took another step through the trees. "Really impressive," she repeated. "Planting that story about the Mocking-bird?" She hesitated and wrinkled her nose as if in thought. "Was that something you came up with on your own? Was it something you were working on? A short story, maybe? A novel?"

"A screenplay," he snapped back. "Yeah. I came up with it. Stay there—don't keep coming closer."

Ella went still, holding out one hand, while still keeping her gun pointed at him. "So help me out... were you the one climbing up behind Jasmine and Maddie—it was you, Maddie, right? In that cave where we found Jasmine? You were wearing your old school uniform, I'm guessing," said Ella.

He looked impressed now, grinning, his white teeth standing out under those black eyes, caught by the flashlight in Brenner's hand.

Ella said, "You kept the polar bear around? Why? I don't get that part. Can you help me? I doubt I'm as clever as you—I couldn't have figured any of this out... But the polar bear was *really, really* cool. I mean, like *wow.*"

He was beaming now, nodding over Maddie's shoulder, chuckling. "Yeah. Pumba, we called him. Dad raised him. Tried out his bait on it, too. Worked, like, crazy good. But man... when I found out my sister was going to be spending time with these little shits? It was like the best coming home present."

"Right... you returned from prison. And your sister was one of the people who wanted to turn you in. Your father didn't like your sister either."

"No... No, he hated them too. For sending me away. But you're right about chumming the tent. I was in that tree. That was something, wasn't it?"

"Oh yeah. Very impressive. You like trees… And a roof, too, right? My friend back there mentioned earlier that he saw a hole in a roof. Did you come through that roof?"

"I can climb pretty good, mhmm. I was like the number one climber in high school. Number one math student too!"

Ella, who'd gone over his record while on the move, had seen no such accolades. But now he was bragging—she had given him what he most desired.

It had bought her some time. Another shuffled step closer. A chance to glance up and around. And then, the moment…

As he talked, chuckling, nodding, his black eyes bobbing like marbles over Maddie's head, his knife lifted, if only for a moment, up and off Maddie's neck. He still kept crouched behind her, using the young woman for cover.

But this was all Ella had needed. A brief moment, a small, temporary opportunity.

Lulled into a false sense of security, she'd given herself a window.

The knife lifted, raised as he gestured about, describing his accolades.

And she aimed and fired. Five bullets in quick succession.

Not at the killer. He was still too close to Maddie. But at the thick branch burdened with snow above him. Two bullets hit the branch. One missed. A third hit another branch. And the last struck the weakened bough. The branch snapped.

Jason Chernow's look of delight shifted to horror, and then his face was lost completely under a small avalanche of collapsing snow. The thick branches, burdened by old snow and new fresh fall, collapsed on him and Maddie.

And Ella burst forward like a gazelle, sprinting desperately.

She flung herself towards the two figures moving about under the snow, desperately trying to crawl out. Ella found Maddie first, yanking her by the arm, pulling her up and out of the snowdrift. "Run!" she said. "Run now! Brenner, help her!"

And then she returned her attention to the ground.

But the second figure was no longer moving. Too deep in the snow... she'd lost sight of him... Where the hell had he gone?

She aimed her gun at the snow, swiveling one way then the other, panting heavily.

A creak... a shift of motion. She turned and fired but something slashed across her leg. She yelled. And then a hand surged up from the snow, snagged her jacket and pulled hard. She collapsed on top of the knife-wielding maniac.

Jason surged from the snow, slashing at her, howling in rage. She missed another shot. He was bleeding from the arm. Bleeding from his leg—the second shot had hit, she guessed.

But her own leg hurt. And he was surging at her with the knife. She was forced to shove his hand down, stumbling back. She traded her gun for his knife. Too close for a firearm anyway. Her weapon hit the snow, but she latched onto his wrist, twisting hard. He screamed in pain as his thumb bent in a shape it wasn't intended to go.

Ella pulled the knife free.

He ducked and snatched one of the branches that had fallen, eyes dead as he stared at her, more snow falling around them like ash from an erupted volcano. He swung his branch at her. It struck her arm. He hit her again. And again. She stumbled with each blow but then used the final shot to step in, taking the impact on her shoulder and slashing with his own knife.

Snow kicked up. And he stumbled back. She slashed again. And he screamed in her face.

"Run! Run!" he yelled in her voice.

Brenner was hurtling towards her now, yelling. Ella ducked a blow with the branch, panting. Adrenaline surging. As they fought, a strange thing seemed to be happening. The more tired they both grew, the more pain they endured, the slower he got.

The faster she got.

The more he screamed, the less she made a sound. The more he bludgeoned at her, trying to crack her skull, the more she moved, feeling an odd, tainted sense of excitement.

"I'll kill you!" he yelled.

But Ella was smiling now. And it haunted her that she didn't quite know why. She avoided a limp-wristed blow with the branch. And she murmured, quiet enough so only he could hear, "If you were going to kill me, you would've done it already."

She ducked back. And he missed again. She slashed him across the wrist and received a howl of pain.

Now the fury on his face was replaced by fear. She taunted him again. "Looking scared there, Jason. Just wait until everyone in Nome finds out what happened here... beaten by a girl. Ouch."

He lashed out again with a yell. But his pride was only flagging him further.

And now, she saw her opening. She stepped in, fast and cold. Her smile slipped; her eyes blazed. She brought her knife against his throat, jabbing the hilt hard into his neck. He choked, gasping as she shoved with the same motion, flipping his legs out, his head back, and slamming him into the snow.

He sprawled and tried to rise, arms flailing, creating a bit of a snow angel... or demon.

And she brought the knife butt to his neck again. He groaned, choking, and his arms went limp. He gasped at the sky, motionless in the ice. The light from Brenner's high-beam shone across them now. Brenner dropped to the killer's side, cuffs in hand. "You okay?" he said.

"Fine," Ella murmured. "Couple of scrapes. Fine... where's Maddie?"

She turned sharply and stared towards where the young, teenage woman was leaning against a tree, shaking horribly, sobbing uncontrollably.

Ella heard the click of handcuffs as Brenner secured their suspect. But Ella didn't look back. The performance simply wasn't worth an *encore*.

And even now, as she hastened towards her cousin's side, Ella heard the rasping voice of Jason... The two blows to his neck hadn't done him any favors. He sounded like a forty-a-day smoker after thirty years of use.

He tried to protest, but Brenner shut him up quickly.

Ella reached Maddie's side, standing next to her.

"Priscilla?" Maddie said, through sobs. "Th-thank you..."

"I'm Ella. I'm... Priscilla's sister. Come with me—we have a fire. You're going to be fine. Are you hurt?"

"Rusted nails. My side. I can't feel my toes."

"Alright. Let's go quick. You're going to be fine, Maddie. Just fine."

The young woman leaned against her cousin's shoulder, limping and hobbling the last leg through the snow, sobbing as if she simply couldn't hold it back.

"I-I'm not usually like this," Maddie gasped.

This struck Ella as such a strange thing to say. She gave her cousin a quick hug and pushed her ahead, towards the waiting fire.

CHAPTER 21

ELLA LET OUT AN exhausted sigh, shutting the car door behind her and pocketing her keys. She exhaled slowly, staring up at the clouds above.

Back in town. Morning, now. The dark gray had turned lighter. The blizzard had passed over the mountains, heading north. But the clouds remained for a while longer.

Ella glanced at her phone, frowning. It had been buzzing in the car. And now she spotted the source of the noise.

Maddie Porter. The contact info said. The text read, *Wanna see my missing toe? Cool right?*

Ella stared at a picture of her cousin's right foot. The pinkie toe was gone. The others, bandaged. A thumbs-up was displayed in the image. Then another picture of Maddie, grinning as if she'd won the lottery.

"What a strange girl," Ella murmured to herself, finding her lips turning up at the corners. She'd spent hours at the hospital with Maddie. Shots, ointments, oils and the like... all of it slapped against the cuts on Maddie's waist.

But according to the doctors, except for the missing pinkie toe, Maddie was expected to make a full recovery.

"Tough girl," Ella murmured, frowning at her phone now as she glanced at another unread text message.

Where would you like to meet?

Her smiled faded, the corners of her lips retreating from their ambitious heights. She glanced over her shoulder, along the street, frowning.

The Graveyard Killer was somewhere in Nome. And he wanted to meet.

The feeling was *not* mutual. She wasn't sure how to avoid him, but for now, she would simply ignore his texts.

She glanced across the street where a police car was parked. Chief Baker's doing. His wife had survived the polar bear, having made it back to Brenner's running snowmobile in time. One of the other cops had been mauled. The bear had gotten away.

Now, Baker had assigned a detail to keep an eye on Ella.

Always watching you.

The message was clear.

But she simply didn't care.

She shook her head, turned, and with a weary sigh, stumbled towards the door. Her replacement clothes, from the hospital gift shop, gave her a sense of guilt. She'd bought them new—breaking her own personal code.

She couldn't wait to slip into something more... her style.

She slipped her keycard into the door, then hesitated, frowning. A cleaning lady was two doors down, smiling at her and then looking away secretively.

Ella blinked. Strange...

She half opened her mouth to call out to the woman. But then exhaustion settled, and she shook her head, pushing through the door.

She stepped into her small motel room, which smelled like a latrine and had stains along the bed. As she slipped in, shut the door behind her, and reached out to find the light switch, she let out a yawn.

The lights turned on.

And she went as still as ice.

A man was laying on her bed. A man looking right at her. He had something in his hand, pointing it towards her. He met her gaze, smiled and said, "Sorry about this."

And then he turned the remote towards the small television on the wall, which was playing a British sports channel. Cricket? Rugby? She didn't know.

She was too busy staring at the *other* man in the room.

The man on the bed had his legs crossed, had fluffed some pillows behind his head, and had even helped himself to a bowl of grapes which he was plucking one at a time and popping into his mouth. The man couldn't have been much older than her father. He had thin hair, but what he did have was neatly combed. When he spoke, he did so with a soft, British accent, that might not have been apparent unless listened to closely.

He was wearing a very neat suit with a red tie and brass buttons perfectly done up. Cuff-links as well.

And next to him—or, more accurately, *under his legs*—was the corpse of another man.

This second man lay lifeless, face down on a white pillow.

The Graveyard Killer looked up, smiling, his gray eyes fixated on her. He adjusted his cuff-links and leaned over, patting the dead man's head.

"Sorry about this. He was here first, though. I think he meant to hurt you..." The Graveyard Killer looked up again, still smiling. Then he gestured at her. "Where are my manners, come in, come in. Would you like a grape?"

She just gaped at the familiar face. The last time she'd seen it, he'd been in the back of her car in cuffs.

Right before she'd let him go.

He was extending a bowl of grapes towards her, still very much using the man he'd clearly killed as a footrest.

The Graveyard Killer just waited patiently, occasionally sneaking a glance at the television screen and wincing or beaming when his team scored a try. Or a wicket. Or whatever the damn sport entailed. He popped another grape into his mouth.

After swallowing and dabbing at his lips with a handkerchief procured from his pocket, he looked up again, and said, "I really don't mean to drop in like this, my dear Eleanor, but time is of the essence. So, please, do come close. We need to chat."

What's Next for Ella Porter?

Girl Wrapped in Branches

A skeleton is found entombed in a hundred-year-old tree, then another, fresher body in a much younger tree.

Is it a century-old killer? Or a family of murderers who've passed their grisly trade down through the generations?

Brilliant FBI Agent Ella Porter, currently banished to the small town of Nome, discovers a woman's remains in an ancient tree and the clues bring her to a small, secluded lake town in the beautiful inland of Alaska. Meanwhile, a wraith from her past wants to forge an unlikely alliance, but some boundaries can't be uncrossed.

Aided by an unwanted informant, as well as her old friend, Brenner Gunn, Ella Porter sets out to solve her most harrowing case yet. Meanwhile, secrets from her past are being unearthed, and threats are closing in.

OTHER BOOKS BY GEORGIA WAGNER

SHE DIES TONIGHT

The skeletons in her closet are twitching... Genius chessmaster and FBI consultant Artemis Blythe swore she'd never return to the misty Cascade Mountains.

Her father—a notorious serial killer, responsible for the deaths of seven women—is now imprisoned, in no small part due to a clue she provided nearly fifteen years ago. And now her father wants his vengeance.

A new serial killer is hunting the wealthy and the elite in the town of Pinelake. Artemis' father claims he knows the identity of the killer, but he'll only tell daughter dearest.

Against her will, she finds herself forced back to her old stomping grounds. Once known as a child chess prodigy, now the locals only think of her as 'The Ghostkiller's' daughter.

In the face of a shamed family name and a brother involved with the Seattle mob, Artemis endeavors to use her tactical genius to solve the baffling case.

Hunting a murderer who strikes without a trace, if she fails, the next skeleton in her closet will be her own.

ALSO BY GEORGIA WAGNER

THE RIVER'S SECRET

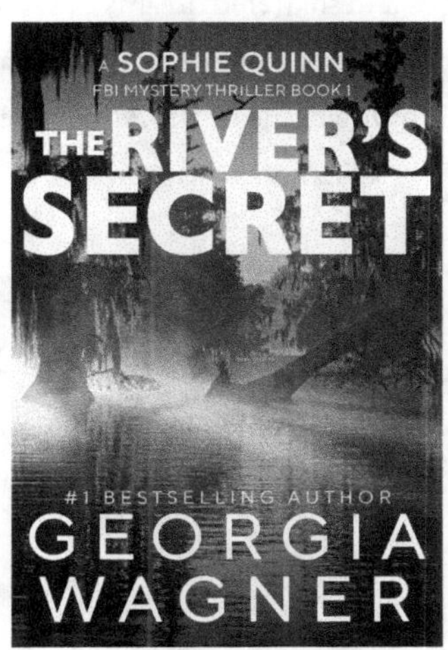

A cold knife, a brutal laugh. Then the odds-defying escape.

Once a hypnotist with her own TV show, now, Sophie Quinn works as a full-time consultant for the FBI. Everything changed six years ago. She can still remember that horrible night. Slated to be the River Killer's tenth victim, she managed to slip her bindings and barely escape where so many others failed. Her sister wasn't so lucky.

And now the killer is back.

Two PHDs later, she's now a rising star at the FBI. Her photographic memory helps solve crimes, but also helps her to never forget. She saw the River Killer's tattoo. She knows what he sounds like. And now, ten years later, he's active again.

Sophie Quinn heads back home to the swamps of Louisiana, along the Mississippi River, intent on evening the score and finding the man who killed her sister. It's been six years since she's been home, though. Broken relationships and shattered dreams exist among the bayous, the rivers, the waterways and swamps of Louisiana; can Sophie find her way home again? Or will she be the River Killer's next victim to float downstream?

Want to know more?

GEORGIA WAGNER

ABOUT THE AUTHOR

Georgia Wagner worked as a ghost writer for many, many years before finally taking the plunge into self-publishing. Location and character are two big factors for Georgia, and getting those right allows the story to flow seamlessly onto the page. And flow it does, because Georgia is so prolific a new term is required to describe the rate at which nerve-tingling stories find their way into print.

When not found attached to a laptop, Georgia likes spending time in local arboretums, among the trees and ponds. An avid cultivator of orchids, begonias, and all things floral, Georgia also has a strong penchant for art, paintings, and sculptures. A many-decades long passion for mystery novels and years of chess tournament experience makes Georgia the perfect person to pen the Artemis Blythe series.